THE JOHNSON COUNTY SHOOTINGS

Regulators Murdoch and Skeeter believe they have an easy assignment hunting down cattle-lifters. But they've ridden into big shooting trouble. Calvin Kingsley, boss of the Circle T, will do anything to become the biggest rancher in the territory. An added danger Murdoch and Skeeter must avoid is a shooting feud between two other ranchers. Aided by an old Missouri guerrilla fighter, they must ensure that Kingsley and his crew pay the deadly price for their law-breaking ways.

ELLIOT CONWAY

THE JOHNSON COUNTY SHOOTINGS

Complete and Unabridged

LINFORD
Leicester

First published in Great Britain in 2005 by
Robert Hale Limited
London

First Linford Edition
published 2006
by arrangement with
Robert Hale Limited
London

British Library CIP Data

Conway, Elliot
   The Johnson County shootings.
   —Large print ed.—
   Linford western library
   1. Western stories
   2. Large type books
   I. Title
   823.9′14 [F]

   ISBN 1–84617–546–1

C1 52904850

Published by
F. A. Thorpe (Publishing)
Anstey, Leicestershire

Set by Words & Graphics Ltd.
Anstey, Leicestershire
Printed and bound in Great Britain by
T. J. International Ltd., Padstow, Cornwall

This book is printed on acid-free paper

For Neil and Doreen Allison
and the fond memories of my
sojourns at Blowick

1

Jeb Sharpe, owner of the Bar Z ranch in Johnson County, Wyoming, strode out on to the porch of his ranch house, his face mottled with murderous rage.

'Your horse is saddled up, boss,' said one of the ranch-hands who were standing outside the big house. 'Do you want some of us to ride into White Oaks with you?'

Sharpe bared his teeth in a death's head grimace of a smile and hefted the double-barrelled shotgun he held in his right hand. 'I've got all the help I need, Jake,' he growled. 'But you boys can get yourselves armed up and patrol the east range. If you see any of that sonuvabitch Warren's crew, shoot 'em down like dogs. Warren started this war again but by hell we'll finish it. This time for good.'

Sharpe swung himself into his saddle

and dug his heels savagely into his horse's ribs, sending it forward in a back-leg dirt kicking start. It had only been twenty minutes since he had seen the grim sight of his straw boss, Slim Cullum, lying tarp-wrapped across his mount's back, shot dead by an unknown ambusher on the trail to White Oaks, or so Sheriff Price had told the boys who had brought Slim's body back to the Bar Z.

Sharpe spat between his mount's ears. He wouldn't believe Price's version of the killing of Slim even if he had the wings of an angel and was holding a Bible. The lying bastard was kin to John Warren and Sharpe remembered his pa telling him, when he had hardly been britched, that rather trust a rattler than a Warren. A week later he was digging a grave for his pa who had been bushwhacked by a bunch of the Warren clan.

It was nigh on three years before the two families slaked their blood-letting. Since then Sharpe had lived through four such-like killing periods. Now, both ranchers were middle-aged and the hot war between them had been running cool for longer than either of them could recollect, though like two timber wolves, snarling and snapping, they were ready to spring at each other's throats at some slight or other.

★ ★ ★

Sheriff Price was sitting on the porch of his office chewing worriedly at his lower lip. Though through his late mother's side of the family he was kin to John Warren, when the regular shooting sprees started up between Warren and Sharpe he didn't take sides, and kept his head down. Duly elected law officer or not, Price knew that if he tried to uphold the peace between the two families, trigger-happy crackpots from either faction would plug him dead. This time though he couldn't hide under his table; he was plumb in the centre of the shooting hell that was about to break out. There was no way Jeb Sharpe would believe that he had not played a part in the killing of his straw boss.

Price felt like bursting into tears as he heaped curses on every male generation of the Warrens and Sharpes right back to the two stubborn, crazy, sonsuvbitches who had fired the first shots in the feud.

To be fair, Price had to admit that if he could catch any of the Bar Z crew breaking the town's law, however slight, such as being drunk and disorderly, discharging pistols in a public place, a bar, the cat house etc, he would throw them in jail. Then he would have the pleasure of seeing the prodding man, Sharpe, or his straw boss, come riding into town to bail out their men, and getting a hard-eyed glare as they handed over the bail due, or losing their men for seven days as they served out their time in the county jail. Favouring the rancher with a shyster's oily, apologetic smile he would say, 'I'm only doing what I'm paid to do, Mr Sharpe, keeping the peace. Any ranch-hand breaking the town's ordinances will see them thrown in my jail. I won't have White Oaks' good citizens' lives being put at risk by wild pistol discharges, or womenfolk molested by drunken horn-dog men.'

Price took a throat-gagging swallow from the whiskey bottle lying handy at his feet and started working on his bottom lip again as he waited for the wild-ass crew of the Bar Z to come fire-balling along Main Street seeking his blood. Then it would be standing-tall time with only a shotgun, as near to his hands as the Dutch-courage bottle, to back him up. He cursed himself for taking the chance of giving Sharpe another prod in the eye.

He had been riding back to town after escorting a prisoner to the county marshal's office in Plainsville and had come across Slim Cullum and two other men of the Bar Z herding in several calves on Double X land.

Crossing over to a neighbour's range to rope in new-born calves that had strayed from their mothers was common and an accepted practice between cattlemen, friendly cattlemen that is. Sharpe and Warren wouldn't pass the time of day with each other even if they were the last men left alive on earth. In fact, their crews had strict orders to shoot on sight any of their rival ranch-hands seen on their range. He had ridden right up to the Bar Z men, catching them unawares, grinning at their surprised looks as he covered them with his rifle.

'You boys ain't partakin' in a spot of cattle-liftin'?' he said. 'Why that's a hangin' offence, Cullum. I'll have to take you into town and put you behind bars till Mr Warren and Mr Sharpe can come to some agreement about just who those young critters belong to. You other two boys can ride back to the Bar Z and let Mr Sharpe know I'm holdin' Cullum as a suspected rustler.'

When Cullum finished dirty-mouthing the sheriff, he spoke to his men. 'You boys ride back and tell the boss what's happened here. I ain't about to cause any trouble, not with a long gun pointin' at us in the hands of an ass-kissin' Warren sonuvabitch.' He cold-eyed Price. 'The trouble will come from Mr Sharpe, a whole damn heap of it. He'll ride out to the county seat and complain that the badge-wearin' bastard in White Oaks is on the Double X's payroll!'

In spite of the heat, Sheriff Price shivered and took another generous swig at the whiskey. Trouble had come all right, fast and unsuspecting. Blood-chilling trouble. Part way to White Oaks where the trail cut through a rocky defile, a rifle shot rang out and Slim Cullum, riding ahead of him was cleared off his saddle, hat dropping off, allowing Price to see the shattered bloody mess that had been the back of the straw boss's head. In one swift, panic-stricken movement he followed the dead man to the dirt, waiting, nerves twanging, for the shot that would kill him. But none came, and he still didn't know why. He did have a fleeting thought that one of the Warren clan was the bushwhacker, but even the Warrens' long-standing hatred of the Sharpes wouldn't have caused them to do something that would leave him right in the middle of shit creek. One thing was for sure, whoever had pulled the trigger, Jeb Sharpe would blame him for deliberately leading his prisoner into an ambush.

The Sheriff breathed a deep sigh of relief when he saw only one rider coming into town: Jeb Sharpe himself. It didn't seem as though it was going to be an odds against him shoot-out. He stood up as the rancher drew up his horse in front of him.

'I'm sorry,' he began. 'But I — '

Sharpe, face all grim lines, cut him off short with a bull-like bellow. 'You're damn right you're sorry! Sorry for carrying out Warren's dirty work! You reckon you don't know who gunned down my foreman but everyone in the territory will know who gunned you down!'

A horrified Price saw the shotgun come swinging over the rancher's chest. His hoarse cry of, 'No!' was drowned by the shattering roar of the gun's discharge. The double blast of lead hail ripped through his shirt and chest with such force that it flung him backwards over his chair and up against the wall of his office and he slid down on the floor in a crumpled heap, his blood flowing dark and freely across the planking.

Sharpe, standing in his stirrups, yelled, 'If any of you folks skulking there in your doorways are kin to that sonuvabitch Warren, tell him I've evened up the score this round, and the shootings have only just started!' He thumbed fresh loads into the shotgun, flicked it shut, then rode back along the street, casting scowling glances right and left as if daring any kin of rancher Warren to try and stop him riding out.

Milt Coster, a bleak-faced, small-built man, sitting on the porch of the Bull's Head saloon, watched Sharpe ride past. Stir things up between Sharpe and Warren, Calvin Kingsley of the Circle T had told him. He looked along the street to where several citizens were crowded around the dead sheriff. Coster smiled, though it didn't soften his features any. He had sure done that, and then some.

It had been a stroke of luck seeing Sheriff Price arrest Sharpe's straw boss and it had taken no sweat to kill Cullum on the trail to White Oaks. He had thought that there would have been accusations and denials passing between the two clans over the killing of Cullum before they started to shoot each other. He had never expected Sharpe to come ass-kicking it in White Oaks with blood in his eyes. His gunning down of the sheriff had really poured coal oil on the fire he had started. He ought to ask Kingsley for a bonus.

Coster, a man sought by the law enforcers of two states, thought, not for for the first time, that hiring out his gun was a damn better paying proposition than sweating his balls off on a cow pony moving around stinking ornery-minded longhorns. Coster turned and walked back into the saloon to spend some of the blood money he had earned so easily.

2

The moon-faced, barrelled-bellied man dressed in a trail-stained black store suit, pants saddle-polished to a mirror-like shine, waddled duck-footed out of the Western Union telegraph office in Billings, Montana, holding a message flimsy in his hand. Hitching his belted pistol holster further round his bulging girth, he gave a grunt and swung himself into his saddle with the slickness of a rider half his weight and age.

'We're about to earn our keep, Skeeter,' he said to his already mounted companion, a narrow-shouldered, foxy-eyed man as small as he was big, wearing a long ragged-fringed buckskin coat, a man who didn't seem to possess the strength to haul out the heavy, long-barrelled pistol he had sheathed, crossdraw style, on his left side. More than a few owlhoots had found out that was a mistaken belief, in the split-second before Skeeter's fast draw shot sent them winging on their way to hell.

'And here's me thinkin' that we were due for a spell of leisure time after cleanin' out that nest of cattle-lifters along the Canadian line[1], Murdoch,' Skeeter growled. 'And with you gettin' plugged an' all. We gettin' put on, you know that, pard? It's as if we're the only goddamned regulators the Cattlemens' Protective Association have on their payroll.' Skeeter was getting into his stride.

'Now, now, Skeeter,' Murdoch broke in. 'There ain't no need to get your dander up. I told you before we sorted out those rustlers that we were gettin' too old to go chasin' after bad-asses. Said that we oughta take up sheep-herdin' or some suchlike less hazardous trade but you wouldn't hear of it. We're takin' the pay so we're obliged to do the

---

[1] The Regulators

job.' Murdoch grinned inwardly. For all his griping he knew that the little hell-raiser wouldn't take up any other calling but regulating. To see that no-good cattle and horse-thieves paid the full price for their stealing ways.

'Yeah, well, m'be so, Murdoch,' grumbled Skeeter. 'But I swear that there's only two sets of men here in Montana, those who own the beef, and the fellas who try to steal it from them.' He favoured Murdoch with a beady-eyed look. 'What bunch of rustlers are we supposed to hunt down now and show them that liftin' cattle will only bring them grief.'

Murdoch waved the wire in front of Skeeter's face. 'Accordin' to this it's a Mrs Gale, owner of the W Y ranch down there in Wyoming, who's havin' trouble with fellas liftin' her stock.'

'A Mrs Gale?' a surprised Skeeter blurted out. 'I didn't think females ran cattle spreads. You're sure the operator didn't make a mistake when he keyed the message?'

Murdoch's bulky frame heaved in a shrug. 'Mrs Gale, that's what it says on this paper and I ain't in a position to doubt it.' Murdoch cleared his throat noisily and looked away from Skeeter before he spoke again. 'The wire also mentions something else, pard, news that ain't goin' to put a smile on your face. Seemingly in Johnson County, that's where this female's ranch is located, there's sort of a range war bein' conducted.'

Skeeter's saddle leather squeaked as he jerked upright on his horse, face twisting in disbelief. 'A sorta range war?' His voice was as high-pitched as a young girl's. 'Are we bein' asked to take part in a blasted range war, Murdoch?'

Murdoch grinned soothingly at Skeeter. 'We ain't expected to get tied up in a range war. All we're ridin' into Johnson County for is to put paid to the no-good sonsuvbitches who are stealin' our client's beef. Now I figure, bein' she's a woman, Mrs Gale won't be runnin' a large herd so I reckon she'll only be losin' fifteen, twenty head at a time. That reasonin' means we ain't about to risk our hides trackin' down a fearsome band of fast-shootin' stompin' men but three, four, local bully boys short of drinkin' and whorin' cash.'

'Could be, Murdoch, could be,' Skeeter admitted grudgingly. 'But that don't ease my mind regardin' that there range war. That kinda war ain't like the regular one we fought in, pard. When we went agin Johnny Reb we knew where his lines were, range war is sneaky killin', night-time, back-shootin' killin'. Whichever side sees our ugly mugs first will finger us as a coupla hired killers workin' for the opposition and we'll get dead. If we do manage to get out what our business in the territory is, our cover will have been blown and more than likely the fellas we're huntin' will hear of it and lie low till we've been pulled out of the county to take up another case.'

'Skeeter,' Murdoch said. 'We've been

pards for a long time and it's always puzzled me why you ain't worried yourself into an early grave frettin' about things that ain't happened. It's me who oughta be doin' the worryin'. You ain't suffered as much as a scratch in all the hairy situations we've found ourselves in, while yours truly has been plugged three times. In fact my right arm is still stiff from the last slug I caught in the line of duty.'

Murdoch grinned. 'Why if it wasn't for your cheerfulness I would have quit this business a while back and bought myself a herd of woollies.' His grin broadened. 'Could be that the W Y crew, bein' their boss is a female, eat real good. I'd ride through a whole heap of range wars to be able to sit down at a table and eat good home-cooked chow, Skeeter.' Po-faced he added, 'M'be eatin' too many warmed-up beans is playin hell with your guts, Skeeter. Filling you up with painful gas, settin' you all grumpy.'

Murdoch jerked at his reins. 'Let's

move out, pard, and make our acquaintance with Mrs Gale of Johnson County, Wyoming.' Grinning again as he heard Skeeter's muttered, 'And m'be goddamned range war,' as he heeled his mount into a trot alongside his.

3

Calvin Kingsley sat on the front porch of the Circle T big house drawing contentedly on a fat Havana cigar. He was in such a good, everything-going-well mood that he had offered one of his special cigars to Matt Duggan, his straw boss, sitting alongside him. If events still ran right for him then the extra cattle he was counting on buying would be eating grass and drinking water at present owned by Jeb Sharpe and John Warren, whose ranches, south of his, ran between the Powder river and its north fork. In a few years time, Kingsley thought hopefully, he would achieve his ambition of being the biggest rancher in Wyoming.

All he had to do was to sit tight until Sharpe and Warren, and their crews, locked in a bloody feud, shot each other up until there weren't enough ranch-hands left to work their spreads. He hadn't started the war; the dispute between the two ranchers was a long standing one about the ownership of a piece of land going back to the days before Wyoming reached statehood. Kingsley slow-smiled to himself. All he had done was to warm up the feud more than somewhat. Leastways, on his orders, Coster had. Six ranch-hands had been killed already in the latest bout of blood-letting between the ranchers and the State governor was threatening to bring in the army and take Warren and Sharpe's land off them and throw them in jail if the killing didn't stop. Kingsley reckoned he ought to be able to buy the two ranches for a song because he was going to make damn sure the mayhem didn't stop.

The other grass and water he needed to fulfil his grand scheme was north of the Circle T, a small spread owned by a widow who bossed over a four-man crew. Duggan was applying the pressure on the widow to quit her land by regularly lifting some of her cattle, beef, or the selling price they were worth, she could ill afford to lose if she wanted to meet the wages and the three squares a day her crew were entitled to.

Duggan, not looking at his boss said, conversationally, 'While we were brandin' on the west range, the widow Gale's boy paid us a call. Warned us to keep our eyes skinned for a bunch of no-good rustlers who were helpin' themselves to his ma's cattle. He reckoned the gang was crossin' over from Montana, doin' their stealin' then high-tailing back over the line. He said the rustlers could ride south and try to lift some of our stock.'

'Well that's right neighbourly of the boy,' replied Kingsley, his gaze directed likewise across his land. Then he grinned and looked at his straw boss. 'I ought to be neighbourly myself, Duggan, like ride over to the W Y and let the widow know how real put out I am hearing that she's been troubled by a bunch of Montana bad-asses after she's sweated her butt off keeping her ranch going since her man died. And not to forget to thank her for warning us about the cattle-thieves.'

'It's a cryin' shame, boss,' Duggan said, 'what trials a poor widow woman has to suffer in this man's land.' His grin was as wide as Kingsley's as he got to his feet. I figure it's time those 'Montana' rustlers lifted a few more of her cows.'

'You do that, Duggan,' Kingsley said. 'But don't take too many. We want her to think it's only a bunch of Montana rough-necks' work. The county marshal won't be keen to waste time and men trying to rope in some out-of-state rustlers if the widow complains to the law about her losses. Him and his deputies have their hands full trying to keep the lid on the big trouble between Warren and Sharpe. We'll wear the widow down, make her realize that running a ranch isn't a female's job. Then as an act of neighbourly charity, I'll offer to buy the place off her.' His wolfish grin showed again. 'Though I figure it won't be worth much being it's plagued by rustlers.' Kingsley sat back in his chair and took a long lung-filling pull at his cigar before relating to Duggan the next moves he intended making to become the biggest rancher in the territory.

'We'll keep prodding at Warren and Sharpe,' he said. 'So as to keep them at each other's throats until the governor carries out his threat and takes over their land.'

His grin this time reached his ears. 'Then that upstanding member of the community, Mr Calvin Kingsley, will step forward and buy the two ranches so that some poor hard-working ranch-hands won't be out of a job.'

'Why that's mighty neighbourly of you, boss,' a straight-faced Duggan said. 'Now I'll round up a few of the boys and pay that call on the W Y.'

4

Murdoch and Skeeter dismounted and tied up their horses on the hitching rail of the only saloon in Alverda, a town two hours' ride from the Montana border. The wire Murdoch had received stated that the W Y ranch was located on the Crazy Woman creek but neither of them knew how far south the creek lay. That information, they hoped, could come from the saloon barkeep, gleaned from him by discreet questioning that didn't raise his curiosity about their business in the territory. Apart from being more dead-eyed accurate with their guns than the rustlers, Murdoch and Skeeter's real edge of being successful thief-takers was by playing the role of a couple of ragged-assed drifters.

They were the only customers in the bar which suited Murdoch. He knew that drinkers in dead-dog towns' saloons craving news from outside the town's limits had all-hearing ears. The barkeep moved along the bar to greet them as they bellied up to it.

It was Murdoch who did the talking. 'Two beers, barkeep, and pull one for yourself.' He waited until the barkeep had placed the beers in front of them before speaking again. 'Me and my pard are aimin' to find us some ranch work hereabouts. We heard there's a ranch along some crick called the Crazy Woman.' He grinned lewdly at the barkeep. 'The only crazy woman we've met was the boss lady of a cat house in Billings up there in Montana when we paid her five dollars short after pleasurin' two of her gals.'

Ranch work? The barkeep had to try hard to keep his hands steady so as not to spill his free drink. He would have laughed out aloud if it hadn't been for the little stranger's off-putting glare. It didn't matter how hard he thought, he couldn't picture the big barrel of lard ass-kicking his pony, swinging a rope to loop in a brush-popping maverick. As for his weedy pard, why he didn't seem to have the strength to pull down and hog-tie a small dog. Not wanting to sicc any trouble on himself he kept his opinions unspoken.

'Yeah, you heard right, gents,' he said to the two would-be 'ranch-hands'. 'There is a cattle spread on the west bank of Crazy Woman crick, thirty, forty minutes' hard ridin' south of here. It's only a small outfit run by a widow woman, a Mrs Gale and a four-man crew so I don't reckon she'll be hirin' extra hands. Further down the Powder is the Circle T, a big ranch bossed over by the go-getter, Mr Calvin Kingsley. He could be needin' more hands.' He gave his two customers another assaying glance with the hint of a sneer in it before adding, 'His crew are a tough, hard-ridin' bunch.'

Murdoch felt Skeeter tense up and guessed that his hair-trigger tempered pard was getting the urge to yank out his big Colt and ram it up the barkeep's nose to knock the cocky look off his face. But they were here for information, not to get thrown into jail by the marshal for causing a disturbance in his town. Before Skeeter could put his thoughts into action he said, 'We were also told that there was a range war goin' on in the territory.'

'You ain't heard wrong, mister,' the barkeep replied. 'There's a real shootin' war goin' on in the south of the county between John Warren of the Double X and Jeb Sharpe of the Bar Z. Though it ain't what a fella would call a range war.'

'It ain't?' said a surprised Skeeter speaking for the first time.

'Naw,' the barkeep replied. 'Those boys ain't fightin' over a section of grass land and a sweet-water crick. The first shootin's started in their grandpappies' time, two bull-headed stompin' men by all accounts, over a piece of dirt a starvin' sodbuster would turn up his nose at. Turned the two families agin each other. For a spell there's been a kinda uneasy peace between them, then something triggers it off and the feud flares up agin into a small war.'

The barkeep took a swallow of his beer, then grinning at Murdoch and Skeeter, said, 'This time it was a real humdinger that set Warren and Sharpe at each other's throats, Sharpe's straw boss was shot by a bushwhacker while Sheriff Price was escortin' him into town after catchin' him red-handed puttin' his boss's mark on a maverick runnin' on Double X land, or so the sheriff later declared.'

'I take it that Sharpe reckoned it was one of Warren's boys who downed his foreman,' Skeeter said.

The barkeep grinned again. 'You've guessed right, mister. Bein' that you're new in the territory, you won't know that Sheriff Price is blood kin to rancher Warren, and Sharpe blamed him for shootin' his straw boss, not some unknown bushwhacker as the sheriff stated, while haulin' him off to jail for a trumped up charge of cold iron work. Sharpe blamed Warren for the whole business and bein' that riled up over the killin' of his man, rode into town and shot Sheriff Price dead as he was standin' on his own front porch. Naturally Warren retaliated. The latest news is four ranch-hands dead and two more badly shot-up. All the mayhem goin' on is giving the county a bad name. There's even talk of the governor bringin' in the soldier boys to put an end to the killin' so I'd advise you not to seek work on those two spreads. It's shoot-on-sight time down there.'

'We sure won't, friend,' Murdoch said. 'Why, me and my pard would ride all day to avoid trouble. Ain't that so, Skeeter?'

'That's right. Why, we ain't shot at anything bigger than varmints,' replied Skeeter, thinking that cattle and horse-thieves could be classified as varmints.

The barkeep believed them. He didn't think either of them had the balls, or the speed with a gun, to face pistol-toting hard men.

After thanking the barkeep for his information on the situation in the county, Murdoch and Skeeter left the saloon to begin their ride south. As they unhitched their horses, Murdoch said, 'We'll be operatin' well clear of that shootin' ruckus, Skeeter, so there's no need to fret any about us gettin' dragged into it.'

Skeeter favoured him with a beady-eyed glare. 'We ain't got there yet,' he grated.

Murdoch grinned. 'It ain't too late for us to quit, Skeeter, and buy us some woollies so we can enjoy our old age. But I opine it wouldn't work out. We're natural-born regulators, risk-takers. If we were to do anything but track down horse and cattle-lifters why we would end up shootin' lumps off each other just to ease the boredom.' He tongue clicked his horse into a long striding walk. 'Let's go and meet that good lady who requires our help and hope she's a good cook and generous with her favours.'

5

Jessica Gale drove the wagon off the main trail and headed towards the branding fire. It wasn't really a ranch chuck wagon she was driving laden with rations, pots and pans and eating irons to feed fifteen or so hungry ranch-hands, but a flat-bed hay cart carrying two freshly baked loaves, a pan of cooked beans and strips of pork, and a pot of hot coffee.

Sam Wright, her leading hand, and Phil Jackson were at the fire doing the branding. Tom, her son, and old Billy Favour, the fourth member of her crew, Jessica reasoned, must be driving the rest of the herd closer to the ranch, as Sam had suggested, before the four of them had ridden out to start the branding.

'If we bed them down in that blind draw, boss,' he had said. 'And mount a two-man guard on the only way in and out we oughta be able to prevent any more of the cows bein' stolen. Up till now those goddamned rustlers have been doin' their stealin' sneaky like, at night. I figure they'll not want to run the gauntlet of two rifles firin' down on them unexpected.'

Any plan that stopped her cattle from being stolen was worth a try, she had thought. She could ill afford to lose any more of her stock — only two days ago another dozen head had been taken — or she would be forced to sell up. Though, in spite of her worries she didn't want Tom, or any of the crew, who were like family to her, to be killed or wounded by the rustlers while protecting the herd.

Jessica knew that she would have no difficulty in finding a buyer for her land. Mr Kingsley of the Circle T had hinted that he was looking for more grass so that he could expand his herd. Then she could buy herself a stretch of growing land, Jessica thought, then sniffed derisively. A female sodbuster no less! But she knew she belonged out here on the great plains, rancher or sodbuster. Living in a town would suffocate her. Kicking on the wagon brake she drew the wagon to a halt at the fire.

'Come and get it, boys, while it's hot!' she called out. 'It isn't time for your regular chow, but I reckon by the time you get the branding finished and the herd bedded down in the draw all you'll want to do when you ride back in will be to flop down on your bunks and sleep.' Jessica grinned. 'That is the two of you who aren't staying out at night to guard the herd.'

Sam and Phil dropped the branding irons and came over to the wagon and helped themselves to the food and coffee.

'It's about time you heard from those regulators the Cattlemen's Association promised to send, boss,' Sam said.

'I was thinking that myself, Sam,' replied Jessica. 'Next time I go to White

Oaks for supplies I'll see if there's a wire from the association waiting for me. They did promise to send me two of their best men.'

Sam had his doubts about that. He didn't think the Association would get themselves all worked up over a small rancher, a female at that, losing a few head of cattle. Not enough to send out their two top men. Only a big cattleman would get that first-class service. Sam's lips hardened. He would settle the rustler trouble himself if he could get the sons-of-bitches framed in the back sight of his Winchester.

★　★　★

'This could be Crazy Woman crick,' Murdoch said, drawing up his horse on the sandy edge of a slow-running clear-water stream, flowing towards a line of trees away to their left that bordered the west bank of the Powder river.

Skeeter heeled his mount over to

where a bunch of longhorns were standing ankle-deep in the water having their fill. He bent low in his saddle to take a closer look at their brands. 'The critters are showin' the WY iron marks, Murdoch,' he said. 'So I reckoned you've figured right.'

'And they'll stay WY cattle, mister! If you two sonsuvbitches make a move towards your guns I'll blow you off your horses!' The shouted threat came from someone behind them.

Murdoch and Skeeter twisted ass in their saddles, Skeeter cursing as he saw who was holding a rifle on them. 'We must be failin', Murdoch,' he muttered. 'Allowin' a young kid to get the drop on us.'

They both heard the ominous double click of a shell being levered into a rifle firing chamber and did some more swinging round on their horses, to see a grey-whiskered old man peering at them along the barrel of a rifle on the far bank of the creek.

'I told you it would only be a coupla

saddle-tramps who were liftin' your ma's cattle, Tom,' Billy Favour shouted. 'I reckon we'll have to find a right sturdy tree to hang that fat bastard from. Though I opine, accordin' to range law, bein' that we caught them red-handed sniffin' around W Y stock we can plug 'em right here and now. It'll save us a whole heap of sweat.'

'You're readin' things wrong here, friend,' Murdoch said. 'Me and my pard ain't cattle-lifters, we're regulators.'

Billy Favour let out a shoulder-shaking horse laugh and his rifle swung slightly off his target. When he brought the rifle back on to the rustlers he found himself eyeballing the twin muzzles of a chopped-down shotgun held as steady as rock in the hands of the fat bastard's partner. And Tom was gazing slack-jawed at the big pistol that had suddenly appeared in the big rustler's fist.

'Now, Mr Gale,' Murdoch said conversationally, 'you can take my word about who I said I was and you and that bloodthirsty old goat can lower your guns and we can talk about the cattle-liftin' your ma's havin', or you can try your luck with us. Kinda see who gets blown into the crick first.' He smiled. 'It's your choice, boy.'

Tom was the first to lower his rifle. The big man knew his name, knew that his ma's cows were being stolen, so, unlikely as it seemed, the pair were regulators. Though they didn't fit his mental image of eagle-eyed, grim-faced rustler-takers.

'It's OK, Billy,' he said. 'Put your gun down, these are the two men Ma's expectin'.'

Billy didn't slip his gun back into its boot but held it across his saddle ready for instant use and to hell with the skinny bum's shotgun. Unlike Tom, he hadn't yet fully accepted that the two ragged-assed characters were regulators. He had seen fellas looking more like regulators being thrown drunk out of saloons.

'I'll take you to my ma,' Tom said. 'I reckon she'll be at the brandin' camp about now with our chow. You stay here, Billy and move those cows into the draw once they've been watered.'

Billy gave a curt nod and wondered how the boss would take it when she clapped eyes on the two so-called regulators.

'That's a sensible move, Mr Gale,' Murdoch said. 'Much better than goin' off at half-cock and sheddin' unnecessary blood.' He smiled broadly. 'Put away that scattergun, Skeeter, our client ain't about to gun us down.'

On the ride back to the camp, Tom kept casting furtive glances at the two regulators to see if he could spot some hidden rustler-catching capabilities in the pair, whatever that would look like, but he ended up with the same disbelieving thoughts about them as Billy Favour. He knew for a fact that his ma would be angry and disappointed on seeing the two men the Association had dumped on her, and after all the years his pa had paid his due to the Association.

★   ★   ★

In no way at all did Jessica Gale think that the two riders coming in with Tom were the men she had been eagerly waiting for. Neither did Sam. Nor did he think they were two down-on-their-luck ranch-hands seeking work.

'Well I'll be durned, boss.' he said. 'It looks like the boy's bringin' in a coupla drifters,' he said. 'They'll be hopin' to sweet-talk you into givin' them a handout, a few dollars to spend in the nearest bar, or some free chow.'

'I don't know what Tom told them, Sam,' replied Jessica. 'But they'll be unlucky as far as a meal's concerned. The big fella looks as though he could eat the best part of a cow at one sitting.'

The trio pulled up at the fire, only Tom dismounting. Murdoch and Skeeter waited, as the protocol of the plains demanded, to be asked to step down.

'These two fellas say they are regulators, Ma,' Tom said.

'Regulators!' Jessica gasped softly, her disbelief of the two riders' profession shown on her face as well as her voice. Behind her, she heard Sam come out with another, 'Well I'll be durned!' in a voice just as unconvinced as she was that the pair were regulators.

Murdoch and Skeeter didn't mind the looks of amazement, shock, whatever their client was giving them. Their appearance was their ace in the hole. It allowed them to fool the men they were hunting, get in close to them until it was too late for the rustlers to do anything about it except mule-skinner curse and raise their hands high, or go down in a blaze of gunfire from the men they tagged as harmless drifters.

'That's right, ma'am,' Murdoch said. 'I'm Murdoch, and my pard here goes by the name of Skeeter.' He reached into his pocket and drew out a folded, well-thumbed piece of paper. 'This states who we are, Mrs Gale and gives us the legal right to do what we're called upon to apprehend the men who are stealin' your stock. You're welcome to read it.'

'And that means shootin' or hangin' them, ma'am,' Skeeter added.

Sam shot the fat rider's partner a sidelong glance and caught a hard-eyed look that cut right through him. Suddenly he had no doubts that the pair were really who they said they were. And, more than that, Sam thought confidently, they could be, as the boss had been told, two top-notch regulators.

Jessica shook her head. 'No it's all right, Mr Murdoch,' she said. 'It was only . . . ' Then Jessica thought how foolish she was sounding. What were regulators supposed to look like? After all, she had never seen any of them before. Then she hurriedly remembered her plainswoman's manners.

'You and Mr Skeeter can step down,'

41

she said. 'I've only brought a snack for my crew but you're welcome to share it. Though if you intend staying the night at the W Y I'll fix you up with a proper meal.'

Murdoch's smile held real warmth as he and Skeeter swung themselves to the ground. 'That would be most appreciated, ma'am,' he said. 'Normally we stay well clear of the folk we're workin' for, bein' that we kinda work undercover so to speak, though I see no harm callin' on you and partakin' of that food you spoke of after dark. Though you and your crew will have to keep our presence on your range to yourselves. We want to rope in the rustlers not to scare them off to do their stealin' somewhere else in the territory. Me and Skeeter will stay out till dark so we can familiarize ourselves with the lie of the land around here. M'be your boy, or one of the crew, could show us what section of your range the cows were taken from.'

Murdoch knew the arrangement would suit Skeeter. His partner's craving for a sit down, home-cooked hot meal was as great as his. Though only half-pint in size he could eat — and drink — him under the table. It could be the last decent meal they'd enjoy for quite a spell for tomorrow they would have to start their hunt for the rustlers in earnest, and that would mean cold night camps and eating iron rations.

'I'll drive back to the ranch, then,' Jessica said, after Murdoch and Skeeter had cleared off in no time at all what Sam knew had been Tom and old Billy's supper. 'You bring Mr Murdoch and Mr Skeeter in when they've finished what they want to do here, Sam.' She smiled at them. 'Don't worry, Sam, I'll cook a meal for four.'

Sam grinned back at her. 'Tom and Billy will be the lucky ones, boss, me and Phil have had chow so we'll stay out and stand the night guard.' He waited until Jessica had driven away from the camp before he gave out his orders.

'Tom, you and Phil finish off here then drive the stock to the draw. There's enough daylight left for me to take Mr Murdoch and Mr Skeeter to where the cows were lifted from. I'll see you later at the herd, Phil.'

⋆   ⋆   ⋆

'This is the northern edge of the W Y range, gents,' Sam said, swinging his arm from a stand of timber several hundred yards ahead of him to a line of low, ragged-topped bluffs. 'Beyond that is open range clear to the Montana border. There's water at those trees though not enough for the whole herd so we bedded down half of them beneath those buttes where there's a pool of spring water. The thievin' sonsuvbitches cut out the number of cows they could handle from that herd. It's hard ground along the foot of those hills stretchin' well northwards. We reckoned the rustlers wanted to hide their tracks. And they sure did that. Old Billy Favour is better than most at tracking but he couldn't cut any sign.' Sam's face hardened. 'The bastards have hit us twice, but we're makin' sure they won't get another chance to lay their hands on the boss's cows.'

'Why would some cattle-liftin'-Montana assholes want to hide their tracks, Skeeter?' Murdoch said, giving his partner a raised-eyebrow quizzical look.

'No reason at all, Murdoch,' Skeeter replied. 'Unless they didn't hail from Montana, but want the folk who they steal the cattle from to think they do.'

Murdoch gave an assenting grunt then looked at Sam. 'If I was a fella with cow-thievin' on my mind with the minimum of risk, I'd take the cows I wanted from the herd you said you had at those trees. It's wide open country out there; I could spot any night rider nursing the herd. I wouldn't take the chance of takin' cattle from the bunch under the bluffs, not on my second raid on the herd. Ranch-hands with cocked rifles could be up there waitin' for me and my buddies to show up.' Murdoch paused, then added, 'Unless I had a pressin' need to do so.'

'What reason would that be, Mr Murdoch?' a puzzled-eyed Sam asked.

'What Skeeter has just said,' replied Murdoch. 'To fool folk. I'll bet my last dollar that the fellas who lifted your boss's cows ain't even seen Montana.'

'Who runs cattle south of the W Y?' Skeeter said.

'Mr Calvin Kingsley, owner of the Circle T,' Sam said. He looked at Skeeter and Murdoch for a few seconds then burst out laughing. 'You ain't considerin' that Kingsley has a hand in stealing our cows, are you? Why he's one of the biggest ranchers in the county, he's got no reason to lift thirty or so head of cattle.'

'That's m'be so,' Murdoch replied, 'but I ain't ever heard of a rancher who didn't crave more grass and water for his stock, especially if he wants to be the number-one rancher in the territory.'

Sam could see no signs of humour showing on the two regulators' faces and his own smile began to fade. 'The sonuvabitch,' he muttered. 'Kingsley showed up at the W Y the other day sayin' how sorry he was to hear we'd been troubled by rustlers and thanked us for warnin' him about them operatin' hereabouts.' He shook his head. 'But I still can't swallow that he's somehow tied in with the rustlers.' Sam pushed back his hat and scratched his head, face twisted with unclear thoughts. 'Though I recollect the boss tellin' me that if she ever wanted to sell up he'd take the place off her hands.'

Skeeter gave Sam another one of his snake-eyed looks. 'What we suspect we keep to ourselves until we get proof, understand? Me and Murdoch have to kinda pussyfoot around this territory to clear up your boss's trouble. We don't want to come out into the open till we're good and ready to slip the nooses around these rustlers' dirty necks.'

'Yeah, I savvy,' Sam said. 'Young Tom can be a mite hotheaded at times and if he thought that Kingsley had anything to do with his ma's cows bein' stolen he'd hightail it to the Circle T, call out Kingsley and get himself dead.'

'Now you've got all the cows boxed in and under guard, Sam,' Murdoch said, 'I don't think you'll have any more stock lifted. If we're right about Kingsley he won't want to risk any of his men bein' killed tryin' another raid and bein' recognized as a Circle T ranch-hand. Then Kingsley would have a lot of explainin' to do.' Murdoch gave Sam a steely-eyed look. 'But don't relax your guard,' he warned. 'If Kingsley is desperate for the W Y land he'll come up with another scheme to force your boss to sell. A dirtier and rougher one.' He smiled at Skeeter. 'I reckon it's time we made that call on Mrs Gale, pard. I swear I can smell that meal cookin'.'

Sam grinned. 'I'll take you to the box draw; Billy will take you to the ranch. The old goat will be ready for some chow as well.'

6

Murdoch, Skeeter and Sam were slow-riding south looking for the tracks of the W Y stolen cattle. Experts in the rounding up of rustlers or not, Sam was thinking that the two regulators had got it wrong. In his opinion the boss's cows were rubbing shoulders with some rancher's stock who wasn't fussy about seeing bills of sale up north in Montana.

Murdoch and Skeeter had been out most of the night and, unbeknown to the W Y straw boss, had cold-camped close to where the cattle were bedded down, ready to back up Sam and Phil if the rustlers did show up. As soon as it was light enough for tired, taut-nerved men to recognize them, they broke camp and rode the short distance to the box draw. Sam, holding his rifle, scrambled down from the ridge to greet them.

'I didn't expect to see you boys up and about so early,' he said.

'Our boss don't pay us to sleep, Sam,' replied Murdoch. 'Me and Skeeter have been out most of the night hopin' that the cattle-lifters would try another raid then we'd have the sonsuvbitches pinned down between four guns. But things don't turn out that easy.' He grinned at Sam. 'Though we had to ride out. After eatin' that grand meal your boss fixed up for us, if we'd spread our bedrolls in that hay barn she said we could sleep in, why, me and Skeeter would have slept for a coupla days. We ain't used to comfort. Isn't that so, pard?'

Skeeter gave a ghost of a smile. 'A kind word would bring tears to our eyes.'

Not used to comfort was the gospel truth, Sam thought. Unwashed, unshaven, trail-stained, wellworn clothes, the pair were looking more like saddle tramps every time he saw them. Only their all-seeing-eyed gazes and the good condition of their horses told him otherwise.

'We're ridin' south, Sam,' Murdoch said, 'hopin' to prove Skeeter's reasonin' that the rustlers are a bunch of fellas hangin' out a lot closer than way up there in Montana.'

'I'll ride with you,' Sam said, 'until we reach the badlands that cuts between the W Y and Circle T ranges. I'll see you at the ranch, Phil.'

  ★   ★   ★

Skeeter, scouting ahead, crisscrossing along a 200-yard front, over land that had changed from lush, cow-feeding grass to a terrain of boulders, cacti and dried-out sandy washes, pulled up his mount on the left of his search pattern.

'I've got 'em!' he yelled.

Murdoch and Sam kneed their horses over to him.

'If those ain't cowpats,' he said, 'then I ain't stepped in one before!'

'The bastards kept the stolen cows close to the bluffs until they had cleared our range,' Sam said, face working in anger. 'Once they reached the badlands there was no need for them to hide their trail thinking that no one would track them south. I owe you gents an apology. Though it still takes some swallowing that Kingsley is a no-good land-grabber.'

'Land-grabbin' ain't in our remit, Sam,' Murdoch said. 'But we'll see Mr Kingsley hang or go to jail, along with his crew, for cattle-liftin'. That's the law, legal and cattlemen's. You can head back to the ranch now to do what your boss is payin' you to do: we'll start doin' what we're paid to do. But not a word to Mrs Gale, or your crew what we know about Kingsley. As far as Mrs Gale's concerned, me and Skeeter are just sniffin' around the territory, OK?'

'OK,' replied Sam. 'But I'd like to be there when the showdown with that sonuvabitch Kingsley comes.'

'If it's possible, Sam,' replied Murdoch. 'Though that ain't-a-hand-on-a-Bible promise. Often events at the end of an assignment move so fast, shootin' and the like, Skeeter and me don't know it's over ourselves.'

Sam gave them a farewell nod and told them to look out for themselves then pulled his horse's head round to ride back to the ranch. Skeeter reached out and stayed his move.

'We've heard there's a range war goin' on here-abouts,' he said. 'Like land-grabbin, range wars ain't what me and Murdoch are paid to settle so we wouldn't like to ride slap bang into the middle of one such-like ruckus.'

Sam grinned. 'There's no likelihood of the pair of you doing that. Sharpe and Warreen, the two feuding ranchers and their crews, are shooting lumps off each other well to the south of Kingsley's range. You might bump into some of the warring boys if you ride into White Oaks, the biggest town this section of the county. Though I've

54

heard that the town's new sheriff, Jeb Sharpe, shot the previous one, has threatened to shoot any of the feuding crews dead if they so much as spit on the boardwalks.'

With another, 'Take care, boys,' Sam jerked at his reins and pulled away from them.

'Let's get down to the business in hand, Skeeter,' Murdoch said. We'll ride across these badlands and take a close look at the Circle T and see if we can come up with a plan of sorts to rope in Kingsley.' He grinned. 'I told you we'd be operatin' well clear of that range war so all we've got to worry about are the normal hazards of our trade, Skeeter, bein' fingered as regulators before we're ready to pounce on the fellas we're huntin'.'

Skeeter beady-eyed him. 'Don't start crowin', pard,' he growled. 'It's early days yet,' then headed his horse into the badlands.

'What do you think of Mr Murdoch and Mr Skeeter,' Billy?' Jessica said, as Billy Favour was saddling up his horse to ride out and relieve Phil and Sam at the draw. 'Last night while they were having their meal,' continued Jessica, 'hearing them talk, I got the impression they weren't a couple of blowhards, seemed that they were capable of stopping the rustlers from stealing any more of my stock. Then looking at them, well . . . ' — Jessica gave a wry grin — 'I had second thoughts.'

'Boss,' said Billy. 'Don't fret any, you were right first time. Those two fellas are good. They fooled me and young Tom when they first showed up. When they told us who they really were I thought that the Association had sicced a coupla over-the-hill operators on you. We had the drop on them thinkin' that they were the rustlers. Then in a blink of an eye the pair of them had their own guns pointing at us, one of them a shotgun. I've never seen slicker moves. I'm glad I ain't one of the cattle-lifters.'

Jessica watched him leave, a great worry was lifted from her mind. The W Y wasn't on their own any more. She turned and walked back inside the house to prepare a meal for Sam and Phil.

7

Murdoch sat at a window table in Foster's eating-house in White Oaks to wait for Skeeter to join him before ordering a meal. Skeeter was still at the livery barn waiting for the blacksmith to show up so he could tell him what kind of shoes he wanted fitting to his horse. There had been only a boy at the barn when they had left their horses there to be fed and watered and rubbed down, and Skeeter hadn't trusted him to pass on to the smith, when he returned from the farm he was working at, that he wanted first-class shoes fitted, and fixed good and true. If it ever came to his having to rely on his mount to get him out of a dangerous situation, Skeeter didn't want his horse to cast an ill-fitted, shoddy-made shoe, slow him and Murdoch down in a life-and-death gallop.

Murdoch beamed at the only other customers in the eating-rooms, two elderly ladies drinking tea. His gentlemanly gesture got him two frozen-eyed looks in return from the ladies who thought that Mr Foster was lowering his standards by allowing, by the state of the big man's clothes, white trash in his place.

'Red savages and drunks will be walking in next, Mabel,' one of the ladies sniffed.

* * *

Murdoch and Skeeter had spent most of the day lying low as close to the Circle T big house and the crew's quarters as it was safe to do so and with the aid of army glasses mentally registered the likeness of all the ranch-hands they saw going about their chores.

'What's the plan, Murdoch?' asked Skeeter.

Murdoch grinned. 'You know we

never make plans, pard. It's the godamned rustlers who think up the plans of how they're goin' to lift some poor rancher's cows. We just try to get in their way when they carry out their thievin' capers. If any of those ugly mugs we've been watchin' show up on W Y grass we have every right to apprehend them as suspected cattle-lifters. Plug the sonsuvbitches dead if they turn awkward. We've got time on our hands bein' that if those boys down there are goin' to do some rustlin', they'll wait until it's dark to do it so we'll ride into this White Oaks place, and have some chow and a beer or two. Show ourselves around somewhat, let the sheriff know we ain't nothin' but a couple of ragged-assed tumbleweeds, that we ain't hired guns workin' for those feudin' ranchers.'

Skeeter was sitting in the shade at the rear of the livery barn enjoying a making when he heard voices in the barn behind him. Thinking that one of the voices he had heard could be the smithy, he got to his feet, stopping suddenly at the door, hand dropping to his pistol as he recognized the voice of one of the men. It was the man he knew who was doing the talking. He drew back and listened.

'I'm tellin' you, Clancey, that big-gutted fella I saw go into that eatin'-house is a regulator!'

'Are you sure, Bubba?' Clancey said.

'Yeah, I'm sure!' replied Bubba. 'That sonuvabitch and his snake-eyed midget of a pard, shot my brother down like a dog when they found cold-iron work on the few head of cattle me and Pat owned across there in the Dakotas. They would have done for me if I hadn't hightailed it out through the back window of the shack and hid in the brush till the pair rode off with all our cows. Now it's my turn to get even.'

'You ain't thinkin' of callin' out this regulator in the middle of town, Bubba?' Clancey said. 'What with this feudin' goin' on, you know the sheriff won't stand for any gunplay in his town. He's got a scattergun totin' deputy patrollin' the street ready to put a sudden end to any shootin' trouble.'

'I ain't in a hurry to gun down the fat bastard,' Bubba said. 'I also want to put paid to his pard, he'll be in town someplace. When the pair get together we'll keep our eyes on them. When they ride out we'll make ourselves known to them along the trail apiece. If they stayin' in town, as soon as it gets dark we'll cut loose at the bastards then ass-kick it outa town.' Bubba cold-smiled. 'Though I've a great urge to hang the pair of them high and watch them dance on air. Once you have seen to your saddle, get hold of Jake and Pete and tell them to go easy on their drinkin', as we might have to be ridin' out sooner than we planned. I'll keep tabs on the fat man.'

Skeeter knew that he had the legal right to step into the barn and get the drop on Bubba, a wanted rustler, and Clancey, shoot them dead if they were desperate enough to make a fight of it.

Then he would have to do some fast talking to the armed deputy, if he didn't blow him away with his shotgun, and his and Murdoch's cover would be blown and it would be goodbye to rounding up the men who were stealing the widow Gale's cows.

Peering through a knothole in the planking, Skeeter saw Bubba walk out of the barn, Clancey took a saddle from a hook on the wall and began working on it. Skeeter padded, soft-footed, away from the rear of the barn before swinging round and heading back along Main Street. Out of the corner of his eye he spotted Bubba poking his head round the corner of a store opposite the eating-house.

Teeth bared in a wolf's snarl of a grin he muttered, 'Bubba, you don't know it yet but you're a walkin' dead man.'

Skeeter's Indian-faced visage when he walked into the eating-house had Murdoch stiffening up in his chair. It told him that serious trouble wasn't far away. The fierce look also upset the two tea-drinking ladies. Leaving their tea they hurriedly got to their feet and made a quick exit from the room, both thinking that Mr Foster was allowing customers in his tea-room who would be thrown out of a decent saloon. Murdoch grinned: his partner's off-putting scowls would have a mad dog crouching and whining with fear.

'What's up, pard?' he asked, as Skeeter sat down at the table. 'You sure scared the hell outa those two females.'

'Bubba Jackson is in town with three of his buddies,' Skeeter said. 'And he knows we're here.'

Murdoch's face screwed up in thought. 'Bubba Jackson? Ain't he the brother of that two-bit cattle-lifter I shot over there in Dakota?'

'That's him,' replied Skeeter. 'The sonuvabitch is just across the street keepin' his eye on us. And by what I heard in the livery barn he's after our blood.'

Murdoch's face hardened as he eased his pistol in its holster. 'Him and his pals ain't reckonin' to gun us down when we step outside on the boardwalk, Skeeter?'

'Naw,' said Skeeter. 'He don't want any trouble with that shotgun-armed deputy prowlin' around the town. He's aimin' to catch us off guard on the trail when we leave town. If we're stayin' the night here, back-shoot us as soon as it's dark. Though he does favour stringin' us up.'

'The sonuvabitch does, does he?' Murdoch said, still stone-faced. 'This is trouble we don't want, Skeeter,' he said softly. 'But it's here and we've got to meet it. Wantin' to hang us could work to our advantage, pard. They'll have to come in close, not gun us down from behind some rocks. Four against two unsuspectin' men, or so the bastards think, will make them cocky, careless-like.' He grinned at Skeeter. 'Before they stop smilin' we'll despatch them on their road to Hell where Bubba can meet up with his no-good brother.'

'But we're aimin' to eat first, ain't

we, Murdoch?' Skeeter pleaded.

'We sure are, pard,' replied Murdoch. 'And partake of a coupla beers as well. We're goin' to act real unsuspectin'-like so Bubba can keep smirkin' at the pleasant thought of how he's goin' to string up a coupla regulators. Right up to the moment when we blow the smirk off his face.'

★ ★ ★

'Here they come, Skeeter,' Murdoch said, as four riders came into sight ahead of them. 'Are you ready?' The double click of the shotgun hammers being drawn back beneath Skeeter's coat told him he had asked an unnecessary question. He was also ready to deal out death fast.

The skirts of his long coat hid his right hand down by his leg, and the long-barrelled .45 Colt pistol it held — a Peacemaker, that fired heavy lead loads that didn't just wing the man they hit but killed him instantly, or tore great holes in his body that made him wish he was dead rather than suffer the few minutes of fearsome agony before dying.

While they had been having a beer in one of White Oaks bars Skeeter had pointed out Clancey to him. 'Bubba will be keepin' out of our sight,' he had said, 'just in case we recognize him.'

He had grinned. 'Ain't he goin' to be surprised then? And I reckon those two weasel-faced gents at the bar are Jake and Pete. I ain't afeared of facin' them in a shoot-out, Skeeter. They don't have the cut of what the Mexes call *pistoleros*. Rollin' drunks in some dark alley is more in their line of work.'

★ ★ ★

'Bubba is still bein' cautious, Murdoch,' Skeeter said. 'He's ridin' at the back of Clancey so we don't spot his ugly mug.'

'Keep smilin', boys,' Bubba said. 'Ya'll give them a polite howdee when we get close, keep them thinking that we're only a bunch of ranch-hands headin' into town for a few beers and a humpin' session. Then, as we pass by them, we get the drop on the bastards. If you have to shoot, only wing them, it's quiet enough out here to hold a double hangin' party.'

'They look a real cheerful bunch,' Murdoch said out of the side of his mouth. 'Let's give them big smiles back to show them that we're really trail friendly. Let them close in for another coupla yards then we'll show them how mean we can be.'

Expert in reading killing-men's minds, Murdoch and Skeeter saw the slight hardening of the outlaws' expressions, saw them spread out to encircle them, and noticed the twitching of their gun hands.

Murdoch did some more side-mouth talk. 'I'll take Clancey and Bubba, you see to the other two. Right, let's start the ball!' His right hand swept upwards, the big Colt flamed and roared. A head shot flung Clancey backwards off his horse, dead before he had cleared his horse's rear. His second shot at a clearly seen Bubba coincided with the deafening boom of Skeeter's shotgun, fired through his coat so Murdoch didn't hear the shot that killed the rustler, only saw his body slump forward across his saddle-horn. The double load of spread shot caught Jake and Pete square in the chest, ripping its destroying way into their flesh. Their spooked horses, rearing and bucking, threw them to the ground to lie along-side Clancey in two crumpled heaps like burst feed sacks.

They both watched Bubba, his mount's feet lifting and kicking as it smelt its dead rider's blood, slide slowly out of his saddle and land face first in the dirt, his left leg trapped in the stirrup iron twisted awkwardly in the air.

'It ain't a joyous sight, Skeeter, seein' our handiwork,' Murdoch said, sober-faced. 'Even though the sonsuvbitches deserved to be shot. But they chose the way it happened.'

'Better we lookin' down at them, Murdoch, than them laughin' down at us,' replied Skeeter.

'True, true,' Murdoch said. Then he sniffed at the air. 'Pard, that fine coat of yours is on fire!'

Skeeter cursed and whipped off his battered hat and beat at the wisp of smoking flame ignited by the shotgun blast spreading across the tail of his hide coat, directing some of his curses at his horse for rearing and bucking.

Murdoch grinned. 'You're long past due gettin' yourself another coat, Skeeter. Though I don't think the Association will refund you the cost bein' what we've just done here is more or less personal business. Nothin' to do with our investigation concernin' the rustlin' of Mrs Gale's cows. Now I reckon it's about time we got back to doin' just that. We ain't got the time to plant those boys and say a few words over their graves. We want to be far away when those bodies are discovered. The sheriff will think that the killin's are linked with the feud that's goin' on hereabouts. It'll not cross his mind that two old farts got the best of four hard men.' He grinned. 'As long as he don't see that burn hole in your coat.'

8

Murdoch and Skeeter were back on W Y land. It had been over ten days since the last raid by the rustlers and the pair were lying in wait on the section of the range from where the cattle had been stolen, hoping that the 'rustlers' could be caught trying another raid and be exposed as Circle T ranch-hands working under their boss's instructions. They sat below a slight ridge wrapped up in their long coats to protect them from the cold wind that blew down from the higher ground behind them; not daring to risk the soothing comfort of makings, the glowing red tips of which would shine like beacons in the tar-barrel dark of the night, giving away their positions to men risking their necks being stretched for cattle-stealing. With cocked rifles resting across their knees, Murdoch and

Skeeter, as they had done on many such-like stake-outs, played the waiting game.

'It ain't much of a plan we've come up with, Skeeter,' Murdoch said, 'but there ain't any other move open to us. No judge would give us a warrant to ride on Mr Kingsley's range and examine his cattle lookin' for altered brands because we suspect that one of the biggest ranchers in the territory is sendin' out his crew to steal his neighbour's cows. He'll tag us as a coupla crazies and wire head office to have us sacked.'

'If a judge did give us the papers to go ahead with our search, Murdoch,' Skeeter said, 'we'd be twenty years older before we checked out every cow that's roamin' on his range.'

'M'be that's so, pard,' replied Murdoch. 'So it looks like we'll have some cold nights ahead of us till — ' Skeeter, raising a warning hand, put an abrupt end to his talking.

'Hear that?' Skeeter said.

'I hear,' replied the big man, his moon-face tightening in hard lines. 'Saddle irons jinglin' if I'm hearin' right.' He got to his feet, Skeeter doing likewise, both holding their Winchesters high, listening and looking intently ahead of them to catch the first glimpse of the darker shapes of the furtive approaching night riders.

'The sonsuvbitches,' Murdoch grunted, 'will be wonderin' where the herd they were goin' to lift a few head from is. We'll split up and have them between our guns, pard. This ain't open range so we have got the right to cut loose at any trespassers, especially those roamin' around in the dark on land that's troubled by rustlers. But just try and wing one so we can nail Kingsley through him.'

They had hardly moved three yards from each other when one of their horses, tethered in a hollow behind them, snorted and neighed. A voice in the blackness in front of them yelled, 'Get to hell out of it, boys, we're ridin' into an ambush!'

Murdoch and Skeeter matched each other in their curses as they fired blindly in the direction of the cries of alarm and the clattering of ass-kicked horses' hoofs. Murdoch thought he heard a rider shout out in pain, but when the pair walked forward cautiously, fingers taking up the first pressure on the triggers of their rifles, to where they judged the raiders had cut and run for it they didn't stumble across any bodies, dead or badly wounded, which brought a fresh stream of curses from the two regulators.

'You lose some, win some, Skeeter,' Murdoch said, making the best of a situation that, through no fault of theirs, had gone sour. 'Leastways we've thrown a scare into the bastards,' he added. 'Oughta put an end to the rustlin', I reckon. As I said before, Kingsley won't want any of his crew killed while attemptin' to steal a widow-woman's cows.'

'It could do,' Skeeter replied. 'But if

we're right about Kingsley set on gettin' hold of this grass, we oughta start worrin' about what the bastard will do next to get his thievin' hands on the W Y land. Though if it ain't cattle-liftin' it ain't exactly our business any more.'

Murdoch cast Skeeter a pain-faced glare as they walked to their mounts. 'Pard,' he said, 'you sure have the knack of dampenin' down a fella's positive thinkin'. But you're wrong about it not bein' our business. Kingsley and his crew are cattle-thieves; there ain't no way gettin' round that. Just because it m'be don't suit him not to do any such-like activities in the future don't make any difference. He stole some of our client's cattle and that's a goddamned fact! And, by hell, Skeeter, I'll see every mother's son of them pay for that, by the rope or gun, or I'll take up nursin' sheep.'

'All right, all right, Murdoch,' Skeeter said. 'Don't get all het up. I didn't say for sure it wasn't our business, I only stated what I thought about the situation. I ain't about to quit on you, pard, there's a lot of loose ends to tie up yet.' He grinned. 'While we're doin' that chore the good widow might ask us to share some more of that fine chow she dishes up.'

★ ★ ★

'They've moved the herd, boss,' Duggan said. 'And we almost rode into an ambush. Whoever was doin' the shootin' put a shell in Peckam's leg, hurt him real bad.' Duggan had roused Kingsley from his sleep thinking that the close shave with death him and the boys had had was serious enough to haul Kingsley out of his bed.

Kingsley, though still in his night-shirt, was wide awake, his mind racing with thoughts of what new tactics he could use to force the widow Gale off her land. Duggan's disturbing news meant that cattle stealing was no longer an option; the risk was too great. He had to keep up his image as a friendly neighbour to the widow; if any of his men were caught stealing her cattle it would end that picture, and his hopes of being the big man in the state. After several minutes of deep thinking he gave Duggan a hard-eyed look.

'Ride into town in the morning,' he said. 'Bring Coster back here, I've got another job for him.'

'And what chore would that be, boss?' a curious Duggan asked.

'Forcing the widow off her land is taking too long,' replied Kingsley. 'Things could be coming to a head between Warren and Sharpe and I want the W Y land before that happens.' He favoured Duggan with an all-toothed humourless smile. 'Now say that the widow's boy was to get tragically shot by those rustlers who have been stealing his ma's cows. I reckon she'll be so full up with grief and shock she would gladly sell the ranch to me thinking that bossing a spread wasn't worth all the pain it had brought her.'

Duggan grinned. 'And that cold-blooded fish, Coster, will be the rustler.'

Kingsley nodded. 'Now let me get back to sleep. I'll see you when you get back with Coster.'

Kingsley lay on his bed thinking that his new plan would work. He was confident that becoming the biggest rancher in Wyoming was within his grasp. He turned over on his side and soon dropped off into an untroubled, dreamless sleep.

Duggan was having thoughts of his own about the way things were shaping up as he walked across to the bunkhouse to grab a few hours' sleep before riding out to White Oaks and hiring a killing man for his boss. Coster had already killed for Kingsley, shooting down the Bar Z foreman, to start up the feud between ranchers Warren and Sharpe again, but the killing of a young boy chewed at him somewhat.

If it ever came public knowledge that he was implicated in the slaying of the widow's boy he would hang for sure.

Though, when he came to think of it, if his cattle-lifting raids came to light he would swing just as high. He had to accept that if you were playing for high stakes, like Kingsley was, then some folk were bound to get stomped on. And he would be up there alongside Kingsley, straw boss of the biggest cattle spread in Wyoming, able to quit night riding stock in thunderstorms and ball-freezing blizzards and get soft-assed sitting in a ranch office handling all the paperwork a big ranch would generate. By the time he had taken off his hat and boots and flopped down on his cot he had convinced himself that any move Kingsley had to make to become the big man in the territory, no matter who it hurt, had to be done.

★　★　★

'Me and Sam heard shooting during the night, Ma,' Tom said, as they both sat down to have breakfast then have a few hours' sleep before starting on the normal ranch chores while Phil and Billy were doing the day watch over the herd. 'Sam thinks Mr Murdoch and Mr Skeeter must have met up with the rustlers.'

'Are they all right?' a worried-looking Mrs Gale asked.

'We don't rightly know, boss,' Sam replied. 'As Tom says, we heard gunfire and took it to be between the regulators and the fellas who are stealing our cows. But we didn't see any sign of the pair on the ride in.' Sam was going to say, 'Or their bodies.' Not wanting to worry his boss more than she was already, he kept that thought to himself, saying instead, 'They'll be OK, that pair can look after themselves.'

'I hope so, I truly hope so, Sam,' Jessica Gale said softly, regretting that she had called in the regulators, painfully realizing that protecting her herd wasn't worth the lives of two good men. Footsteps sounding on the porch allayed her feelings regarding the wellbeing of Mr Murdoch and Mr

Skeeter. The two regulators stood at the open door, smiling, waiting to be asked into the house. She ran across to welcome them in. 'I was becoming 'feared for you both,' she said. 'Sam and Tom told me that they heard shooting last night. Were you involved in a gunfight with the rustlers?'

'That's right, ma'am,' Murdoch replied. 'Me and Skeeter surprised them and sorta discouraged them from doin' what they had on their minds. You ought not to loose any more stock bein' that the rustlers have lost their edge of surprise. They'll not want to risk sheddin' their blood tryin' to steal a few longhorns.'

'That means your work here is finished,' Mrs Gale said. 'That's a big relief to me. I didn't want either of you coming to harm on my behalf. You must have a meal before you ride out. Just sit down; I'll set two extra places at the table.'

'That's mighty charitable of you, ma'am,' replied Murdoch. 'Me and

Skeeter can always do justice to a good meal though we ain't leavin' just yet. The rustlers could still be in the territory fixin' to steal some other rancher's cows and until we put paid to them our job here ain't done. After we eat we'll snatch a few hours' sleep in your hay barn then set out to hunt down those cattle-thieves.' Murdoch grinned. 'If we don't clear up this situation now, in a few weeks' time we could be makin' the long trip here from Montana again to sort out a cattle-stealing problem.'

Mrs Gale gave a gasped, 'Oh!' Then she gave a forced smile. 'At least I'll see you both eat well, when you find time to, while you're here on W Y land.'

She received genuine ear-to-ear appreciative grins from Murdoch and Skeeter.

After breakfast, Murdoch said that he and Skeeter would tend to their horses then rest up for a spell before taking up watching the comings and goings at the Circle T.

'I'll water and feed your horses,' Tom said. He grinned. 'You two old gents get your heads down, us younkers don't need as much sleep.'

Murdoch looked at Skeeter. 'We're gettin' spoilt here, pard.'

'Ain't that the truth,' replied Skeeter, still savourin' the fine breakfast he had downed. 'And gettin' paid as well.'

When Tom led the horses away and the regulators had Sam on his own, their faces lost their easy-going looks.

'You tell him the bad news, Skeeter,' Murdoch said. 'It's your reasonin'.'

'What bad news is that?' a quizzical-eyed Sam asked.

'There ain't any doubt in either of our minds that Kingsley's behind the rustlin',' Skeeter began 'because he wants the W Y land. He thought the land would come his way by liftin' your boss's cattle. Kingsley won't risk stealin' any more, but the way I see it, if he still has the urge for this range he'll come up with other schemes to get the widow off her land.'

'Such as, Skeeter?' Sam asked, his good-humoured mood also gone.

'Barn burnin', torchin' the ranch house, m'be back-shootin' some of the crew,' Skeeter replied. 'It depends on how desperate Kingsley is to get hold of the W Y grass and water.'

Sam's face whitened. 'He wouldn't do that, would he, kill one of us?' disbelief sounding in his voice.

'Believe it, friend,' Murdoch said. 'Big ranchers tend to make their own laws, be their own judge and jury. Down there in Texas and New Mexico the gringo cattlemen shoot Mexes, Injuns and whites to hang on to what they originally grabbed from the poor Mexes. Why, here in your own back yard, two ranchers have declared war on each other just because they don't like each other, and the law can't stop them. Kingsley has a reason for what he's done to the widow and he'll stoop as low as he has to, to succeed. Keep a close guard on the house, but don't let Mrs Gale know how we see things. Just tell your crew to be on the alert for any bushwhackers.'

Sam looked at the hard, set faces of the two regulators and believed.

'I'll warn them that we ain't trouble free yet,' he said. 'And to watch their backs as they go about their business.' Sam thin-smiled. 'I was going to lay down my weary head for a spell but you fellas' comfortin' words have knocked all the tiredness outa me. I don't know how you two manage to sleep considerin' all the hassle your trade brings you. Sweet dreams anyway. I'll see you before you ride out.'

* * *

It was late afternoon and Murdoch and Skeeter were back on the trail to resume their watch on the Circle T.

'Skeeter,' Murdoch said suddenly. 'I've been ponderin' over the situation we have here and I came up with a wild-ass thought, one you ain't goin' to favour if it makes sense to you.'

'Pard, most of your thoughts upset me somewhat,' replied Skeeter. 'What you told me about this business back there in Billings didn't give me joyous thoughts. But as you told me there we get paid to clean up bad situations.' Still po-faced he added, 'I reckon you're about to tell me that you think Kingsley started up the present shootin' trouble between Sharpe and Warren.'

Murdoch gazed slack-jawed at Skeeter. 'Well I'll be durned!' he gasped. 'You've read my mind.'

Skeeter grinned at his partner. 'It don't take a genius to figure out that if Kingsley gets hold of the widow's land he ain't goin' to be a much bigger rancher than he his right now. If the sonuvabitch has growin' big ambitions he'll not settle for anything less than ownin' Sharpe and Warren's spreads. It's in his interest to have them fightin' each other. He'll just sit back and wait until the army steps in and throws the pair in jail, if they're still alive.'

Skeeter's beady-eyed look returned. 'And we could still be dragged into that feud you stated we'll stay well clear of.'

'I can't deny I said that, pard,' replied Murdoch. 'But it ain't goin' that way, not by a long chalk. Though I was thinkin' that if we can prove to Sharpe and Warren that Kingsley started this round of shootin' they could be willin' to help us to rope in Kingsley and his boys. That would sure give us the edge over the Circle T crew.'

Skeeter gave a snarl of a laugh. 'I ain't reckonin' to be a Daniel stridin' into a lion's den. 'Cause that's what we'll be doin' if we step on to those two ranchers' lands. It's itchy-trigger-finger time on those ranges. We'd be shot well and truly dead before we could make it to the big house to tell them what we suspect. Me and you, Murdoch, are the regulators here and it's beholden to us to clear up that widow's trouble. OK?'

'You're right, Skeeter,' Murdoch said.

'We're the paid thief-takers. We'll stay well clear of that ruckus.' Though, he thought, fate, ill-luck, whatever, could decide otherwise. Murdoch kept that sober thought to himself.

9

'Take a look at that fella who's just come out of the ranch house with Kingsley,' Murdoch said, handing the army glasses across to Skeeter. They were lying, bellies hugging the dirt, behind the same observation ridge overlooking the Circle T main buildings.

Skeeter took a calculating look at the man shaking hands with the ranch owner. He was a small, shut-faced man and, as he swung into his saddle, Skeeter noted he favoured the wearing of two sheathed pistols. 'He ain't no ranch-hand that's for sure, Murdoch,' he said, keeping the glasses on the twogun man as he rode out. 'A hired gun, I reckon.'

'My reasonin' exactly,' replied Murdoch. 'No cow hand would waste his hard-earned due on an extra pistol, not while there's heart-warmin' liquor and females to be had. Kingsley's steppin' up his ante for the W Y land. You trail that two-gun fella, Skeeter, it looks as though he's headin' towards White Oaks, you ain't as conspicious lookin' as me. Find out what you can about him. I'll stay on lookout till you come back.' He grinned. 'Have a beer for me while you're there.'

★ ★ ★

Skeeter had no trouble finding the whereabouts of the two-pistol man in White Oaks. If he and Murdoch had guessed right about the man's profession, Kingsley would have paid him well. All he had to do was to see outside of which saloon the gunman's horse, a black with white forefeet, was tethered. Though, when Skeeter did come across the horse, it was tied up outside the priciest of the two cat houses White Oaks had.

It figured, Skeeter thought, hired

guns were a blow-hard breed. When they were in the money they splashed out the dollars somewhat just to show that they were a cut above ranch-hands and bent-backed sodbusters. Though cow hands and farmers generally passed over in their old age, with their boots off.

Skeeter's eyes glinted cold and hard. That hired gun lying on a bouncy spring bed in an upstairs room sporting with a high-priced whore would definitely have a short life if he harmed the widow woman or her boy. He, Oliver LeRoy Skeets, would see to that. Then Skeeter put aside his solemn vow and concentrated on the business he was in White Oaks for, to find out all he could about the two-pistol man And he knew it wasn't going to be easy.

He couldn't go asking questions about him in the saloons in case the hired gun got wind of it and called him out for poking his nose into something that wasn't his business. That, Skeeter thought, would put him real deep in that dog-dirt creek as the townsfolk would be wondering how a fella who had the appearance of a ragged-assed bum could out-gun a man who could handle two pistols at once. Pertinent questions would be asked by the law and his and Murdoch's cover could be in jeopardy.

Kingsley had struck some sort of a deal with the man inside the sporting house, and whatever it was it would be directed against the W Y. What was the son-of-a-bitch's name? If he knew the gunman's name maybe he could find out if he ran with a bunch of like-minded buddies. Then he and Murdoch would know how big a threat they were facing. The gunman's horse caught Skeeter's eye again and his face ceased its twisting and scowling. With one quick slash of his knife a grinning Skeeter cut through the horse's tethering rope.

A hang-dog-faced Skeeter walked into the sporting house, and got a down-the-nose glare from the big-breasted blonde sitting at the reception desk as though some varmint, a skunk or a possum, had crept into the building. For one appalled moment the blonde thought that the little foxy-faced bum, dressed in clothes that ought to have been burnt years ago, was going to ask for the services of one of the girls.

Her quick, but expert assaying of the ragged-dressed man told her he was not some panhandler just come down from the hills with bags of gold dust in his pockets to whoop it up in town, but that he was exactly what he looked like, a broken down, unwashed bum. Her hand reached for the small bell on the table to summon one of the sporting house bouncers out front to kick the little saddle-tramp's butt into the street before he caused a stink in the place.

Skeeter favoured the blonde with a smile that somehow sent shivers running up and down her back. She had seen starving wolves with friendlier looks. She lifted up the bell then held it in mid air, as the old man spoke.

'I'm sorry to bother you, ma'am,' Skeeter said. 'But I came across this horse wanderin' down the street a piece. Is it likely the critter belongs to one of your clients? Or should I take it along to the sheriff's office?' Skeeter's fearsome grin flashed again and once more the blonde got that uncomfortable feeling. 'I sure don't want to be strung up for horse-thievin', ma'am. It's a black with white forelegs.'

'It belongs to Mr Coster!' the blonde snapped. 'Its hitching rope must have worked loose.' Which wasn't surprising how fast Coster had come into the place wanting to get to bed with Gloria before any other client booked her. Then, for some unexplained reason, the blonde felt a pang of sympathy towards the elderly down-and-out. 'Here, take this,' she said and handed Skeeter a silver dollar. 'Tie the horse back on to the rail then go and get yourself a beer.' Better still, the blonde thought, get a long hot soak and a shave.

A grinning Skeeter came out of the cat house bouncing the silver piece in his hand. And Murdoch said he hadn't a way with women.

★　★　★

Murdoch heard a slight rustling of grass behind him, but didn't make a frantic grab for his rifle lying next to his right hand. It could only be Skeeter coming back in. Only his partner could move so silently. Murdoch firmly believed that somewhere back along Skeeter's family tree, there would be a full-blood Indian whose skill at tracking and pussy-footing around had been passed on to Skeeter.

'That fella with the two guns goes by the name of Coster,' Skeeter said, as he flopped down alongside Murdoch. 'And as far as I could find out he's a loner. Right now he's enjoyin' himself in a high-priced bawdy house. Kingsley must have paid him a killin' fee.'

'Well, that ain't bad news, Skeeter,'

replied Murdoch. 'We've only got one man to keep our eyes on.' His face clouded over. 'Though I'll have to admit that this assignment ain't as straightforward as I told you it would be back there in Billings. It's not like our usual job of work where we have a good idea who the cattle-lifters are and all we've got to do is to find where they are holed-up and deal with them. All we can do is to stay on the alert for that gunman to make his play, then jump him.'

'Kingsley might not just sit back and let his hired gun earn his pay,' Skeeter said. 'He could take a hand in the game himself. Then we'd run outa eyes tryin' to watch them all.'

'Unless,' Murdoch said, his face lightening up, 'we take a leaf outa Kingsley's book and do some raidin' ourselves, such as raidin' the Circle T. It ain't like we're breakin' the law, Skeeter, bein' that Kingsley and his crew are low-down cattle-thieves. If we hit him hard it should put his mind off whatever trouble he m'be plannin' against the W Y.' He grinned. 'That's if you don't mind gettin' shot at by the Circle T crew.'

'Why should I mind, pard?' replied Skeeter. 'We're paid to expect bein' shot at by rustlers, ain't we? It's gettin' plugged by fellas I've no beef with that I don't take kindly to.' It was Skeeter's turn to smile. 'Besides it's only right that we should be doin' something to help our client considerin' that fine chow she put before us.'

'Let's head back to the W Y then,' Murdoch said, getting on to his feet. 'And explain our thinkin' to Sam and his crew. See if they think we're crazy.'

10

Sam and Billy Favour were all set to start the nightly guard of the ranch house and the closest of the outbuildings when Murdoch and Skeeter rode in. Murdoch wasted no time in telling the two ranch-hands how Kingsley had got himself a hired gun. Sam swore softly, Billy not so quietly.

'Mr Murdoch,' Sam said despondently, 'Kingsley's got us beat. All of us are standing night watches, me and Billy here, young Tom and Phil at the herd. We're managing to get a little shut eye during the day, in between doing the normal ranch chores, now, if we've got to watch each others' backs in the daytime all of us will be too bushed inside a week to eat our chow let alone do any work.'

'It ain't as bad as it looks, Sam,' Skeeter said. 'We reckon Kingsley won't raid you, he'll let the hired gun do his work. And that sonuvabitch will do it in daylight so you can catch up on your sleep.'

'That's welcome news, Skeeter,' replied Sam with some feeling. 'Even the boss is sitting up most of the night with a shotgun laid across her knees.' He gave the two regulators a narrow-eyed questioning look. 'Are you sure about Kingsley's men not coming fireballin' in?'

'You can bet your horse and saddle on it, friend,' Skeeter said. He smiled. 'Ain't that so, pard?' Then Murdoch smiled, nodding in agreement.

And Sam, who had once scouted for the army in the Big Horn campaigns after the Custer massacre, swore that he had seen more heart-warming looks on the Sioux and Crow hostiles they had captured. Still having his doubts, he asked why they were so sure about Kingsley not raiding them.

'Because me and Murdoch intend to do some raidin' of our own,' Skeeter replied. 'Such as scatterin' Kingsley's cows to points far away. That should keep his crew busy close to home for a spell and give us time to scotch that hired gun's play.'

'Ain't that somewhat out of your line of business?' a surprised Sam asked. 'Bein' regulators an' all.'

'What me and Skeeter are goin' to do, Sam,' Murdoch said, 'is to raid a nest of cattle-thieves which by any law, the state's or the cattlemen's unwritten one, is sure legal.'

Billy Favour saying, 'Stampedin' Kingsley's herd ain't goin' to win you much time, Murdoch,' put an end to the discussion of the legality or otherwise of raiding the Circle T.

'The cows won't scatter far; Kingsley's home range is enclosed by hills,' Billy continued. 'And he's got a big crew to round them up. Now if you were to burn down the bunkhouse — better still, the big house — that's something that'll give the sonuvabitch a real headache and keep him at home.'

Billy gave a gap-toothed grin. 'And bein' I've had experience in such-like activities I'd like to ride with you gents just to see if I ain't forgot my old trade. If you and the boss don't mind that is.'

Straight-faced, all polite like, Skeeter said, 'If it ain't too personal to ask, Mr Favour, how came you by this old 'trade' of yours?'

Billy's grin widened. 'I once rode with a bunch of the wildest boys you ever did see, bossed over by a genuine stompin' man by the name of Quantrill way down there in the Kansas border country, burnin' out free-staters long before we Rebs took you blue bellies on in the big war.'

Just as straight-faced as Skeeter, Sam said, 'Why the old goat showed up here ten, eleven years ago and I took pity on him looking all played out and ragged-assed and signed him on the payroll. Now I find out that me, a God-fearing Yankee, have hired a Missouri fire-raisin' brush boy. Why, me and the rest of the crew could have been burnt to death in our beds! You're welcome to ride with Skeeter and Murdoch, Billy, and light a fire under Kingsley's ass.'

Billy looked pleadingly at the regulators. Murdoch got a slight agreeing nod from Skeeter in answer to his glance at him.

'Mr Favour,' he said. 'Bein' that me and my pard are a couple of new boys in the burnin'-out trade, and we ain't vain, proud men, it would be downright churlish and foolish not to accept the offer of an expert fire-raiser. You can prevent us from burnin' our fingers.' He smiled. 'And catch some of the lead that could be flyin' around.'

Billy flashed his broken-toothed grin again. 'Just give me a few minutes, friends, till I get me some coal oil. In the old days when we burnt out some freeslaver, a dozen or so of us would ride in, shootin' and a-hollerin', all of us totin' lighted torches, but naturally we can't do it that way here. But we can't spend all night lightin' matches to start a blaze only yards from the ranch's main buildin's, there's bound to be night riders nosin' around. By usin' coal oil we can get a real fire goin' in no time at all and be ridin' out before Kingsley knows what the hell's happenin'.'

'There's food ready on the table, Mr Murdoch!' Mrs Gale called out from the house porch. 'If you've got the time to sit down and eat it!'

'Thank you, ma'am,' replied Murdoch. 'Me and Skeeter will always find time to partake of a good meal.' He looked at Billy. 'Mr Favour, you get what you need to start a real July the Fourth fire at the Circle T. We'll ride out when me and Skeeter have had our chow, OK?'

Billy grinned. 'I'll give you a burnin' out at Kingsley's old Quantrill, if he had still been alive, would have been right proud of, or my name ain't Billy Favour.'

★ ★ ★

A dim, flickering storm lantern hung above a doorway of a long single-storeyed building that the would-be fire-raisers took to be the crew's quarters, but there were no lights showing in the big house windows. Murdoch and Skeeter had brought Billy Favour much closer to the ranch house than the ridge from where they had first spied on the ranch.

'So far so good,' Murdoch said. 'Now it's up to you, Mr Favour. But if you raise the alarm you get to hell out of it fast, understand? We don't want Kingsley to recognize you as a W Y hand or he and his boys will swoop down on the W Y and do some burnin' out of their own. Me and Skeeter will cover you and if the worst comes to pass to anyone in the territory but you folk at the WY, we're just a coupla no-good drifters.'

'Murdoch,' replied Billy. 'Kingsley, or those boys lyin' asleep in that bunkhouse won't see my ass for dust if any shootin' starts. I won't even stop to jump on to my horse.'

'Bein' we've settled the plan of action,' Skeeter said, 'where do you intend to start the blaze, Mr Favour?'

Without any hesitation Billy pointed to a dark, low-shaped building which was vaguely visible by the light from a star-filled sky almost abutting the ranch house.

'That'll be the woodshed,' he said. 'Start a blaze in there and the way the wind is blowin' the flames will reach under the porch of Kingsley's fine house in no time at all. And I can light the fire under cover.'

The moon suddenly cleared a patch of cloud and the whole scene in front them became as clear as though it was daytime.

Murdoch cursed. 'Do you see them?' he growled.

'I see them,' replied Skeeter. 'Two men at that horse corral. You oughta know, pard, that no job comes easy to us.'

'There'll be recently born foals with

those horses,' Billy said. 'Those men there to guard them just in case wolves come roamin' down from the hills and start to worry them.'

'One of them's movin',' Skeeter said. 'He seems to be doin' the circuit of the corral.'

'Time him, Skeeter,' Murdoch said.

The three saw the patrolling guard come into view round the right-hand corner of the corral, saw him stop and exchange a few words with the man guarding the stockade gate before he set off on his round again.

'Ten minutes, maximum, I reckon, Murdoch,' Skeeter said.

'Can you start your blaze and get back here within that time, Mr Favour?' Murdoch said.

'It'll be a rush job, but I can manage it,' replied Billy. 'But it's that fella at the gate that's got me worried. In this goddamned moonlight he'll pick me out crossin' that open ground right in front of his nose.'

Murdoch grinned reassuringly at

Billy. 'Skeeter will see to it that he's no problem.'

Billy shook the can of coal oil. 'I'm rarin' to go,' he said. 'I'm feelin' like it was in the old days.' He grinned. 'And here's me thinkin' I'd took up with religion.'

Then the night favoured the fire-raiser; the clouds hid the moon again.

'The plan's just the same,' Murdoch told Billy. The guard might not be able to see you now but he could hear you. You make your way down to that clump of brush and keep an eye on that guard. When he goes down you get on with startin' your fire.'

Billy looked round to wish Skeeter good luck and that he hoped he would see him later but discovered that the little regulator was no longer with them in the trees.

'That pard of yours, Murdoch, sure moves light-footed,' he said. 'Has he got Injun blood in him?'

'He reckons he ain't,' replied Murdoch. 'All I know is that right now he'll be within cold-cockin' range of that guard down there. And, as I said, when he drops you . . . ' Murdoch stopped speaking, realizing he was talking to himself. Then he opined that ex-Missouri brush boys moved just as sneaky-like as any Indian.

He lay down on the ground and brought his rifle to his shoulder, aiming it at the door of the bunkhouse from where, if things went sour, trouble would come boiling out. Skeeter would see to any mishap at the corral. They could do no more to back up the old raider.

Billy crouched down low in the brush, eyeing the guard. He was gasping for breath like some broken-winded horse, finding out how long ago were the old days. Billy forced himself to breathe more regularly; he had made a promise to the two regulators and Sam, and himself, that he would start a fire and trusted that his pride would pull him through.

By the acrid smell of the leaves and

soil, Billy guessed that the patch of brush was used by the Circle T to relieve their bladders during the night rather than make the trip to the ranch crapper. Billy thin-smiled. He hoped to hell that none of those asleep there in the bunkhouse would wake up with an urgent need to have a piss.

On the next time around, the patrolling guard stayed a little longer talking to his partner, both of them lighting up cigarettes. Billy did some praying and mule-skinner-type cursing. If he had to stay squatted here much longer when the time came to do his work he would be hobbling across to the woodshed, and his high hopes of starting the fire within Murdoch's stated time would have been an empty promise. Then, as if an answer to his prayers — or curses — the picket guard moved off.

He had hardly been swallowed up in the darkness when Billy saw the other guard's dim silhoutte sink out of his sight, the burning red end of his makings arcing to the ground. Billy surprised himself by haring across to the woodshed as though it was in the old days.

Skeeter dragged the body of the unconscious guard into the corral and stepped through the bars and sat, back against the gate and lit a cigarette. He still held the long-barrelled Colt he had used to lay out the guard, thinking that if the old raider didn't live up to his words, the next time he used his Colt would be for the task it was intended, the discharging of death-dealing lead — the start of one hell of an odds-against-him gunfight.

Billy found he hadn't lost his old skills. On entering the woodshed he discovered it was half full with split log lengths to fuel the fires of the big house. More in his favour there was no wall at the end of the shed facing the house, nothing to stop the flames sweeping out to reach the underside of the roof of the back porch. Billy, sweating and trembling as though he had done several hours of back-breaking chores, began pouring the coal oil on the logs stacked at the open end of the shed, making sure he splashed some of it on the wooden floor of the porch only a few feet away. What oil was left in the can he used to make a trail as he walked backwards to the door. A match that had been gripped ready between his teeth was struck into flame on the butt of his pistol and applied to the trail. Billy smiled with satisfied pleasure as he watched the fiery trail burning fast and unhindered towards the oil-soaked logs.

Once out of the shed, Billy put his hand to his mouth and let out the mournful hoot of an owl, the old signal of the brush boys telling that what had to be done was done and it was getting-to-hell-out-of-it-fast time. Billy hoped that Skeeter would understand the signal. He waited, the sweat drying cold on him, with a cocked pistol fisted until he picked out the small shape of the regulator closing in on him. He gave Skeeter a nod and a grin then the pair of them set off at a run to join Murdoch at the rendezvous. He paused long enough to look round and see flames shooting out the shed which, as Billy had surmised, fanned by the strong winds, were already licking under the porch roof. Billy gave Skeeter another grin.

'It's a damn sight more excitin' than tendin' cows.'

Skeeter grinned back. 'M'be so,' he replied. 'But there ain't much callin' nowadays for burnin' out gents. Now let's get back to Murdoch and make ourselves scarce.'

Murdoch also saw the flames and gave one of his moon-faced smiles. The old goat and Skeeter had pulled it off! He'd had no doubts that his partner would fulfil his role in the enterprise. He could ride through Hell itself and come out with old Nick's fork slung across his saddle. They had worked together for over ten years, knew each other's thoughts in a backs-to-the-wall situation, and acted accordingly, an expertise that had saved their lives several times over.

Billy Favour had proved himself, but in the dangerous trade he and Skeeter followed, it didn't do to risk your life on some man's opinion of his capabilities. His partner had done just that. But he had been worrying for nothing. He owed Mr William Favour a silent apology. Murdoch stood up and, holding his rifle across his waist, he watched and listened for the return of the two fire-raisers.

'Good work, Mr Favour,' he said, as the pair of them came stumbling over the rise. 'It's time we weren't here, gents. Though I reckon the Circle T crew will be too busy tryin' to put out that fine fire you've lit, Mr Favour, for Kingsley to send out his boys to hunt down the fellers responsible.'

They mounted up, but stayed a few minutes watching the chaos below them, half-dressed men tumbling out of the bunkhouse, men forming a bucket chain in a vain attempt to douse the high-reaching flames.

'You've done your bit, Mr Favour, to take Mr Kingsley's mind off tryin' to get his hands on the W Y, now it's up to me and Skeeter to prevent that hired gun from doin' his killin'. We'll ride back to town and keep a check on him.'

'You go back to tendin' those cows,' grinned Skeeter. 'You've had enough excitement for one night. And don't tell Mrs Gale or the boy that you've gone back to your old raidin' ways. If Kingsley takes it in his head to ride out to the WY seekin' any information about who could have started the blaze I want them to show real surprise at the news. They can't lie as good as us old farts.'

Billy pulled his mount's head round and, before heeling it in the ribs, he said, 'You gents take care now. It's been a pleasure riding alongside you.'

Murdoch and Skeeter watched Billy ride out then they dogged him for a few hundred yards before turning to swing wide of the blazing house and headed towards White Oaks.

A crazy-eyed, smoke-blackened Kingsley angrily shouted out orders to his crew urging them to make greater efforts to put out the fire before it engulfed the whole house.

'What sonsuvbitches did this?' he snarled at Duggan. 'Was it the WY crew having cottoned on to the fact that we were responsible for stealing their cows?'

Duggan, as smoke grimed as his boss, shook his head. 'New,' he replied. 'The men, at least two of them, the one who cracked Josh's head open, and the bastard who started the fire, knew their business. The widow's crew are ranch-hands, one of them is a young kid, another an old man. And I can't see a woman giving out orders to burn you out. Naw, we'll have to look further afield for the fire-raisers than the WY, boss.'

Then Duggan had a disturbing thought. Could it be Sharpe or Warren's work, thinking that the Circle

T had sided with either one of them? Kingsley would have to contact the ranchers to tell them that their feuding was no business of his. Though not right now, not while Kingsley was watching his fine house going up in flames. He was naturally tetchy at the moment, could shoot him dead out of hand just to take it out on someone for all the frustrated anger bottled up inside him.

To ease his own tight-assed-nerved feelings he yelled, 'Hurry up with those goddamned buckets before the whole place burns down!'

* * *

Murdoch and Skeeter had made camp on the outskirts of White Oaks only riding into town when it came to life, and the eating-house was open for business. While Murdoch was finishing his meal, Skeeter did the searching for Coster. Ten minutes later he came back into the eating-house and by the way he was scowling, Murdoch knew that his partner's seeking out of the hired gun hadn't been successful.

'We're too late, Murdoch,' Skeeter snapped. 'Accordin' to the swamper at the saloon across the street the bastard rode outa town last night.'

A bleak-faced Murdoch pushed back his chair and stood up, losing the taste for the remainder of his breakfast. 'The sonuvabitch is keen to earn his pay,' he said. 'It's time we did some trackin' and earn our due, Skeeter, or we'll sure fall outa favour with that nice widow lady.'

11

Milt Coster, lying behind a rock, got a clear view of his target, the widow rancher's son, and put his rifle to his shoulder, ready to draw a bead on him as soon as he came into range. He wondered who Kingsley would want him to gun down next. Milt was beginning to see the reason behind his killing of the Bar Z straw boss and now the kid, but it was no business of his. As long as the Circle T boss came up with the ante he'd be happy to kill anyone Kingsley cared to name. He smiled. It was like money from home: no sweat money.

Tom, riding out to check on one of the waterholes, glimpsed a brief sun-reflecting flash on the hillside away to his left and remembered Sam's warning before he left the ranch to keep a sharp lookout for trouble. The

119

warning had puzzled him.

'Didn't Mr Murdoch tell us that him and Mr Skeeter had chased off the rustlers?' he had said.

Sam still hadn't told Tom and his mother that Kingsley was behind the rustling and that the gunman he had hired could be roaming close by, but he knew that Tom had to be warned to keep on the alert. 'It's just a precaution, Tom,' he lied. 'Those rustlers having been stopped from lifting your ma's cows could move south to do their stealing on Circle T land. You don't want to bump into a mean bunch of cattle-lifters.'

Again Tom saw the ominous glint and by some warning instinct he didn't know he had, he flung himself out of his saddle and the Winchester shell aimed to blow his head to bloody pieces shattered his left shoulder instead. He heard the crack of the rifle through the waves of sickening pain as he hit the dirt. He landed heavily on his wounded arm and gave out an agonized cry then, mercifully, he blacked out.

* * *

As they approached the house Murdoch and Skeeter saw that Sam was talking to a tall, thin man wearing a long-coated black suit: a man they hadn't seen before. The tall man got into a buggy and pulled away before they reached the house.

They had hardly drawn up their mounts when Sam, face as hard as flint, blurted out, 'Young Tom's been shot! That sonuvabitch Kingsley's hired gun bushwhacked the kid at the south water-hole. According to the doc — he was the fella in the buggy — the boy will be OK. But if Billy hadn't spotted Tom's horse wandering about, the boy could have bled to death. Naturally the boss is all shook up; she thinks the rustlers have come back, and she's all set to sell the place to Kingsley. I haven't told her yet that Kingsley is the bastard causing all her trouble.'

'I'll do that, Sam,' Murdoch said. 'It was down to me and Skeeter to keep tabs on that hired gun, but we didn't find out till this morning that the bastard had pulled out of town last night.'

'And I'll tell you this, friend,' Skeeter said, in a matter-of-fact voice, though his cold-eyed gaze sent Sam's blood running cold. 'The next time that fella leaves White Oaks he'll be nailed in a wooden box making the short one-way trip to Boot Hill. And you have my word on that.'

An ashen-faced Mrs Gale stepped out on to the porch and Murdoch and Skeeter got an accusing glare that caused them to twist ass uncomfortably in their saddles. 'He's sleeping peacefully now, Sam,' she said. Then, plucking up her courage, she looked directly at Murdoch and Skeeter. 'I thought that you told me we would have no more trouble with the rustlers, Mr Murdoch?' she said angrily. 'This morning they almost killed my boy!'

'Me and Skeeter are right sorry to hear that the boy's been shot, ma'am,' Murdoch said. 'And we're glad to know that he's goin' to be OK. It's also time you knew what's goin' on on your land.' He then told the widow about Kingsley's men doing the rustling and his hiring of the gunman who shot her son. 'Kingsley's been doin' all that to pressure you to sell your land to him, ma'am,' Murdoch finished off.

Jessica Gale stood wide-eyed with disbelief for a moment or two, unable to speak as she took in what Murdoch had told her. 'Kingsley? My neighbour?' she managed to finally gasp, her voice still showing her doubts that a man she and her late husband had known for a long time, could have paid someone to kill her son. 'How could he do this to me, Mr Murdoch?'

'Greed, ma'am, greed and wantin' power,' replied Murdoch. 'But me and Skeeter have kinda reined Kingsley in somewhat. As you know we put paid to the so-called rustlers. Then, just to stop him from sendin' his crew on to your range to cause more trouble for you, Skeeter and Mr Favour put a torch to Kingsley's big house last night.'

'Old Billy!' Mrs Gale gasped. 'Setting fire to Mr Kingsley's fine house?'

Murdoch grinned. 'That's right, ma'am. You don't know what hell-raisers you have on your payroll.' Then, face serious again, he said, 'Me and Skeeter rode to White Oaks to try and track down the gunman but we didn't find out till this mornin' that he had left town last night, as your boy painfully found out. But as Skeeter has just told Sam, that sonuv — beg your pardin' ma'am, will do no more bushwhackin'.' Murdoch was going to say, 'this side of Hell's gates,' but being told that he and Skeeter were cold-bloodedly contemplating killing a man, was something a God-fearing lady shouldn't hear. Though, on reflection, having her only son almost shot dead the widow would be mad keen to plug the man who fired the shot herself.

'I am sorry I was angry with you, Mr Murdoch,' Jessica said, 'But with Tom lying there I-I'm just a bundle of nerves.' She gave a wan smile. 'I'm just a worried sick widow and still can't believe what you have just told me about Kingsley.'

'That ain't all the skulduggery Kingsley's been up to, ma'am,' Skeeter said. 'Me and Murdoch believe that his hired gun not only shot your boy but shot Sharpe's straw boss as well, so the sheriff would get the blame. And him bein' kin to Warren, Sharpe took the bait and started off the feud again.'

Both Jessica and Sam gave shocked, disbelieving looks.

Skeeter serious-eyed Sam. 'Mr Kingsley is thinkin' big, Sam. He'll not be satisfied with just takin' over this parcel of land. He has a strong hankerin' for every blade of grass and water source in the whole county.'

'What can we do to stop him?' a worried Mrs Gale asked. 'Alert the sheriff to what he's up to?'

Murdoch shook his head. 'We've no proof that will stand up in a court of law, ma'am, that Kingsley is responsible for your troubles.' He gave what he hoped was a reassuring smile. 'Leave it to me and Skeeter to bring Kingsley to book.'

'Forgive me for forgetting my manners,' a flustered Mrs Gale said. 'There's food on the table if you want to eat. I can't guarantee it will still be warm but you're both welcome to it.' The smile she gave them had some life in it.

Murdoch turned in his saddle to ask Skeeter if he was going to take up Mrs Gale's offer but a grinning Skeeter was already swinging down from his horse.

'Twenty minutes here or there won't harm our business in White Oaks, Murdoch. And besides, we oughta pass the time of day with the shot-up boy.'

* * *

126

While Murdoch and Skeeter were mounting their horses to make the vengeance trip to White Oaks, Sam asked them if they were going to bushwhack the gunman. Murdoch favoured Sam with a hurt-eyed look.

'Me and Skeeter ain't a coupla no-good back-shooters,' he said. 'Skeeter will give him a chance to draw his pistol in a face-to-face shoot-out. Ain't that so, pard?'

Skeeter didn't answer, only smiling a cat's-got-the-cream smirk, leaving Sam to think, as the pair rode out, that if Skeeter could pull out a Colt pistol as fast as Billy had told him he'd hauled out a shotgun from God knows where, then the 'fair' chance the gunman would be getting was the same odds as a greenhorn's chance of winning the pot in a poker game against a professional tinhorn gambler.

12

'That's the sonuvabitch's horse, Murdoch,' Skeeter said, as they slow rode along Main Street, 'tied up outside the whorehouse, the place he was in when I came seekin' him. It seems that the 'sins of the flesh', as the Good Book puts it, come before tendin' to the needs of his mount.'

Murdoch thin-smiled. 'Well he ain't likely a character who'd be sittin' at home with his boots off readin' his Bible. Though it suits us him bein' there. He could be spendin' his ill-come-by gains in a saloon and we'd have to get set up for long time wait till we could get him on his own.'

They drew up their mounts outside the sporting house, Murdoch giving the building a long calculating look before dismounting. 'OK, pard,' he said. 'Let's go and make ourselves known to him.'

'You ain't got any soul, Murdoch,' Skeeter grinned. 'Interruptin' a fella when he's raisin' a sweat with some purty gal.'

'Not for any bushwhacker who guns down kids, I ain't,' Murdoch growled, as side by side, they strode purposefully into the whorehouse.

'Sweet Jesus!' the blonde at the desk gasped. 'There's two of the bastards!' The little weasel-faced bum's partner was as big as he was ugly. His black suit was so creased and stained with wear the town bum wouldn't be seen wearing it even when drunk. And the big ape had the cheek to be favouring her with a wide, moon-faced, stupid grin. Why the hell couldn't one of the other girls be at the desk? She didn't like turning customers away but she was making an exception with these two creeps. Not bothering to give the pair a forked-tongued welcoming smile, she reached out for the bell to summon the bouncer, forgetting that he only came on duty when the night trade picked up.

Murdoch stepped up to the desk sharply and his ham-like hand grabbed the blonde's arm, firmly, but not tight enough to hurt her. The blonde looked up; the big ape's grin had vanished and his ball-of-lard face had hardened and lengthened. She cast a nervous glance at the little weed and saw the same frightening look in his features. He wasn't the same man she had given the silver dollar to. Whoever they were they were definitely not work-shy drifters. And she prided herself on being able to read men's characters. She gave a silent cynical laugh — maybe only when they were stretched out buck-naked in her bed.

'Me and my pard, missee,' Murdoch said, 'have some pressin' business to conduct with one of your clients, a Mr Coster. We know he's in here, we saw his horse tied up outside. You just oblige us with the number of the room he's havin' his pleasure in and we'll have words with him then be on our way in no time at all.' Murdoch flashed his big grin at the blonde again.

The girl fixed-gazed Murdoch with the mesmerized intensity of a jack-rabbit eyeballing a rattler. She had a gut feeling that the words the pair were going to have with Coster would be coming out of the barrels of the big pistols they had strapped about their middles. She had never taken a liking to Coster. He fancied himself as a ladies' man, a big spender and a genuine hard man, but he had a streak of viciousness about him that scared her and she was glad it wasn't her he was bouncing around the bed. Coster, the blonde thought, was going to get the chance to show just how much of a hard man he really was. She worried only about Gloria, the girl with him.

Murdoch gave her another one of his beaming smiles. 'The room number?' he repeated, soft-voiced.

The blonde got a grip on her nerves. 'Room four, second room on the right, up the stairs,' she managed to get out.

131

'Mr Coster won't be too happy having his session with Gloria interrupted.' Then, plucking up courage, she added, 'Will she be OK?'

Skeeter gave her what he opined was a reassuring smile which only set the blonde's nerves jumping again. 'Why shouldn't she be?' he said. 'Our business is with Coster.'

It was with some relief the blonde watched them walk up the stairs. She believed what the little man had told her. Whatever trouble was about to break out in that room, Gloria would come to no harm.

The pair stopped outside Coster's room, listening for a moment or two, then Murdoch gave Skeeter a slight nod. Skeeter hurried, cat-footed, along the hall to the glass door that opened out on to the balcony they had eyed from the street, that ran round the four sides of the building. He stepped outside and walked along the balcony and halted at the corner of the rear wall. One of the six windows he could see would be the one Coster would come scrambling through when Murdoch opened up the ball — that's if their plan worked. He drew out his pistol and held it down by his side.

Murdoch, reckoning that Skeeter would be in position by now, pulled out his own pistol and hammered on the door with it, yelling, 'It's the law, Coster! I'm holdin' papers on you for two counts of murder! I know you're in there, I've seen your horse tied up outside. Just step out peaceful like and the girl won't get hurt!'

Coster jerked up like a spring uncurling. The redhead rolled off him and off the bed, landing on the floor with a painful thump that caused her to cry out. A dirty-mouthing Coster grabbed a pistol from his gunbelt hanging on the bed end and fanned off three shots at the door. The redhead shrieked in fear and, jaybird-naked, she rolled right under the bed. Coster leaped to his feet and, scooping up his discarded clothes, made a flying dash for the window, wondering as he did so how the hell the Montana law had tracked him to White Oaks here in Wyoming. It couldn't be the local law — as far as they knew he was a law-abiding citizen.

Murdoch grim-smiled. His bluff had worked. He had assumed the gunman would be wanted by the law someplace. By Coster's rapid and lethal reaction the law-breaking he had committed was serious enough for him to shoot it out with a man he thought was a state marshal. It had been a wise decision to keep well clear of the door after he had hammered on it.

On hearing the shots, Skeeter thumbed back the hammer of the Colt and held it resting on his right shoulder, all ready to throw down on Coster when he made his appearance. Giving the gunman a fair chance didn't mean giving him any edge.

The third window scraped open. Skeeter smiled for real. First he saw two red flannel-drawered legs reaching for the floor of the porch, then an arm holding a pistol, then the whole of Coster came into sight, anger-flushed face looking which way and every way. Coster saw Skeeter and the anger changed to fear as he did some more dirty-mouthing. He swung his pistol on to his new threat but was too late by a lifetime. Skeeter threw down on him and triggered off one shot that put a red weeping eye in Coster's brow, a killing shot. Clothes, boots and pistol dropped out of dead hands as Coster staggered back and fell across the window ledge he had hopefully thought would have been his escape route.

Murdoch, recognizing the deeper boom of Skeeter's .45, opened the door and stepped into the room. He saw Coster's body at the window, half in, half out of the room. He had the limp, boneless appearance of a man whose next trip would be to Boot Hill and he sheathed his pistol. He heard sobbing from under the bed and glimpsed a wild-eyed frightened face — and the glistening whiteness of naked female flesh, more than he had seen for a long time.

'It's OK, missee,' he said. 'The shootin's over, you can come on out.'

Sniffing back her tears, the redhead shuffled under the bed until she could reach out a hand to pull a sheet from the bed. With a lot of twisting and turning she managed to wrap the sheet round her. Only then did she roll out and stand in front of Murdoch.

'Can I go now?' she said, still fear-eyed.

'Of course you can,' replied Murdoch in a fatherly, comforting voice. 'We've done what we came here to do.'

The girl bent down to pick up her clothes laid across the back of a chair when a voice from the window said, 'You'd better take this, Red.'

The girl gave a startled cry and swung round in time to see her late client's body being pushed aside to hit the floor with a dull thud, and a little man dressed like the French 'breed mountain men who came in to winter in the settlement she had lived in as a child.

Skeeter came right up to her and handed her a thick wad of dollar bills held together by a piece of cord. 'Coster ain't got no more use for spendin' money,' he said. 'And we don't need it. But bein' that we kinda threw a scare into you it's only right you should have it.' He grinned. 'I reckon you're only gettin' it somewhat faster and with less sweat than you would have earned it.' Skeeter glanced across at Murdoch. 'It's time we were skedaddlin', pard, before we have to let the sheriff know why we're here in his bailiwick.'

Skeeter was right, Murdoch thought. To explain their shooting of Coster to the sheriff they would have to break their cover. And there was no guarantee the sheriff would keep their being Association agents to himself. Then their chances of roping in Kingsley on cattle-lifting charges would be gone; he would lead the life of a saint while they were in the territory.

The redhead came to a quick decision, and solved Murdoch and Skeeter's problem. The big man and his little partner were not the same cut of men like that dead asshole, Coster. They no longer scared her. She knew that none of the men who had paid for her services would have done what the little man had done. The sons-of-bitches would have kept the money for themselves.

'The last door on the left along the hall opens on to the back stairs,' she said. 'They lead down to the kitchen. There'll be no one in there this early so you can go out by the back way unseen.' The redhead gave a weak grin. 'I'll have a fit of hysterics when the sheriff shows up; that ought to keep him occupied till you can sneak round to the front and get your horses.'

Murdoch touched his hat in a salute to the girl. 'Missee,' he said, 'It's been nice to have made your acquaintance.' He grinned. 'I'm only sorry I ain't got the time for you to make it a pleasure.'

'You take care now, gents,' the redhead called after them, as the pair walked out of the room, then, hurriedly, she began to get dressed.

At the sound of the shooting, the girls had dashed into one of the back rooms and locked the door behind them. They were paid to entertain men, not to get lumps shot out of them by wild-assed ranch-hands. Only the blonde stayed put at the desk, worrying about Gloria and sucking her blood-trickling thumb. She had been doing her nails when the gunfire shattered the quietness of the house and she had jabbed the file into her thumb with shock. Gloria, running down the stairs, all smiles, had her jumping to her feet, a surprised look on her face and her sore thumb forgotten.

'Are you all right, Gloria?' she cried. 'I heard shooting . . .'

Gloria didn't stop her grinning. She showed the blonde the roll of bills. 'That's what happened, Belle!' she said, then told her all that had happened in the room.

Belle shook her head in disbelief. 'At first I thought the little fella was just a worthless drifter,' she said, 'but when he came in with his big pard and asked what room Coster was in I took them for a couple of hard cases.' She laughed. 'Now they've turned out to be two fast-shooting, kind-hearted uncles. It shows you how wrong you can be, Gloria, putting tags on fellas.'

Gloria stuffed the roll down the front of her dress. 'I'll split it up among all of you when the boss isn't around, and after I've done my act with the sheriff. I promised I'd keep him tied up while they get to their horses. The pair of them must be keeping low in the side alley till it's safe for them to make their move.'

Deputy Sheriff Bilby was sitting in the sheriff's seat, sweating blood, wishing that the sheriff hadn't left him in charge of the office while he was away for the day on personal business.

140

He had heard the sounds of gunfire along at the whorehouse and, as a man paid to keep the peace in town, it was his given duty to go along there to find out what the shooting was all about. And he would have done so. He would have walked, bold-assed, along the boardwalk to the sporting house carrying his shotgun, loaded in both barrels, like a real old-time frontier town-tamer, if Mr Sharpe of the Bar Z and six of his boys hadn't been drinking in the saloon. Some of them, unbeknown to him, could have paid a visit to the whorehouse and met up with a bunch of the Double X crew already there doing their humping and started the feuding for real again.

Bilby heard no more shooting so he took a chance, one he had to take if he wanted to continue being a deputy sheriff. He loaded his shotgun, jammed on his hat and left the office, not feeling bold-assed at all. He was trying not to think too deeply the morbid thought that the reason there had been no more gunfire was because the feuding crews were sneaking around each other, each trying to get the edge over their rivals before starting up the shooting again.

When a foot-dragging, dry-throated Bilby stepped into the whorehouse, he saw Gloria, bawling her head off being comforted by big Blondie. In secret Bilby lusted after both of the girls but couldn't afford their prices, not on a deputy sheriff's pay and wife and two, always hungry, kids to support.

Gloria lifted her head off Belle's shoulder and favoured Bilby with a moist-eyed, pity-poor-me look. The sudden fire in Bilby's loins put steel in his back, expanding his chest and the tin shield on his chest almost seemed to glow. By heck, he thought, gripping the shotgun tighter, why he'd blow even Sharpe to hell and beyond if he had caused those tears to flow in that pretty redhaired girl's eyes.

'Oh, Deputy!' she sobbed, 'There's been a shooting! I was entertaining Mr Coster in my room upstairs when two men burst in and shot him dead.' Then she began to cry again and rested her head back on Belle's shoulder.

Deputy Sheriff Bilby wished fervently that the redhead had rested her head on his shoulder so that he could put a comforting arm around her. Then he remembered the reason he was here. The girls were relying on him to protect them. He wasn't shedding any tears over the killing of Coster. An asshole like him had made a lot of enemies. In fact, he had been ordered by the sheriff to keep a wary eye on Mr Coster. 'That fella,' the sheriff had told him, 'splashed out a lot of money he don't seem to work for.'

'Are the shooters still in the building?' he asked. 'I saw a coupla horses tied up outside when I came in.'

'No, they left straight away after they had shot Coster,' replied Belle. 'And they were strangers. They just came in and asked me as polite as you like what room Coster was in.'

'Did you get a good look at the pair,

Blondie?' Bilby said.

'We sure did, Mr Bilby,' Blondie replied. 'They were about your build. One of them had a black beard, and his pard had a knife scar running down his right cheek. Isn't that right, Gloria?'

'That's them right enough, Belle,' sniffed Gloria. 'They had the cut of hired guns, Mr Bilby.'

'You girls stay put,' Deputy Bilby said, in a walking tall voice. 'You're in no danger now. Give me the number of your room, Red, and I'll check that Coster is really dead.'

As soon as Bilby had walked up the stairs and disappeared from their view Gloria ran out on to the front porch and called in a low but carrying voice, 'It's OK for you to get your horses, gents. Me and Belle will stall the marshal for a few more minutes so that you can get well clear of the town. Not that it matters, he don't know what the pair of you really look like. And thanks again for the cash!' She walked back inside and kept a watch for the sheriff

144

to come down the stairs.

She smiled at Belle when they heard the jingling sound of saddle irons and the soft padding of horses' hoofs in the dust of Main Street.

13

Duggan, in charge of the crew who had brought back a wagonload of timber for the rebuilding of the fire-damaged ranch house from White Oaks, told Kingsley about the killing of Coster. 'Two fellas, strangers in the territory, boss,' he said. 'Shot him while he was playing around with a whore in the cat house. It's also going around the town that the doc had been out to the WY to treat the widow's boy for a bad arm wound. So it seems that Coster earned his pay before he was plugged.'

Kingsley only vaguely heard his straw boss telling him about the boy being shot. He was trying to puzzle out who had killed Coster. If his house hadn't been set on fire he would have guessed that the gunman had met his end by men like himself, hired guns, men who had caught up with him in White Oaks and settled an old score they'd had with him.

He was getting an uneasy feeling that the fire and Coster's violent end were not some coincidental happenings but were linked somehow. Kingsley gazed past the wagon, looking, but not seeing, face working in a mixture of emotions, puzzlement, anger, and something Duggan had never seen on his boss's face before, the glint of fear. Fear of what, the straw boss thought?

Then Duggan began to do some thinking of his own. Two men, at least, were responsible for torching the ranch house, two men gunned down Coster. He couldn't see any connection. But still he noticed that the shooting of Coster had somehow set Kingsley worrying. Duggan gave the situation some more pounding over as he stepped down from the wagon and gave orders to unload it. What he came up with had him showing some fear of his own.

What if the four men were part of a

gang of vigilantes who had somehow got wind of the fact that the Circle T were cattle-thieves? And they must have known Coster had killed for Kingsley and they had shot him. The vigilantes dished out the law as prescribed by Judge Lynch, death by the rope or bullet with no appeals being heard. But who were these merciless bastards? The W Y crew? They couldn't be any of Sharpe, or Warren's men they had their hands full killing each other. Grim-faced, he felt an uncomfortable tightness around his neck. He was going to ask Kingsley if he was having the same wild thoughts but he had stepped back into the house. His high hopes of being the straw boss of the biggest spread in Wyoming didn't look so rosy now.

★　★　★

Murdoch and Skeeter had made camp just off the main trail between White Oaks and the Circle T land on what they believed, seeing no longhorns grazing, was open range. From now on it would be a waiting game for them, watching to see if Kingsley made any further aggressive moves against the W Y. A plan that didn't go down well with Skeeter.

'The way I see it, Murdoch,' he said. 'Our job here is finished. Kingsley can't risk lifting the widow's cows and he sure won't hire another gunman. Though I'll admit things ain't turned out as clean cut as I'd have liked. The rustlers ain't dead or waitin' to be strung up.'

'Yeah that's true, pard,' replied Murdoch. 'I know we can't stay here for ever watchin' Kingsley, but I've got a bad feelin' about that sonuvabitch. His twisted pride won't let him give up on what we think his ambition is, Skeeter. As sure as I'm sittin' jawin' to you, that sonuvabitch will make one last attempt to force Mrs Gale off her land. We'll keep our eyes on the Circle T for another week and if seems that

Kingsley is happy with the water and grass he already owns we'll head back to Montana and report back in. But not before we say our farewells to the W Y.' Murdoch grinned. 'M'be that fine widow woman will fix us up with one last meal, to kinda see us on our way, so to speak.'

Skeeter's growled, 'We've got visitors!' shifted the smile off Murdoch's face. Twisting round he saw the riders, seven of them, coming across from the main trail towards them. 'They could be sociable-minded gents, coming in to pass the time of day with us,' he said, not very convincingly.

Skeeter gave him a sour-faced look. 'Yeah, and I'm old Abe Lincoln's long lost son.' He stood up, but not before he had slipped the short-barrelled shotgun into one of the pockets of his long coat. Murdoch heaved himself up from the ground and tugged his holstered Colt's pistol a few inches across his great belly, giving him a split-second faster draw, time that could keep them alive if the riders closing in on the camp were bringing trouble with them.

'None of them look to be sportin' tin stars, Skeeter,' Murdoch said quietly. 'So it don't seem they're a sheriff's posse seekin' out those two desperados who plugged Coster. So we ain't got anything to worry about, as long as we both keep smilin' and talk polite like.'

Skeeter, narrow-eyeing the incoming horsemen, cut loose with a string of curses. 'Murdoch,' he said, 'remember tellin' me that we'd stay well clear of that range war bein' conducted hereabouts? Well, I hate to tell you but you got it all wrong, because I reckon we're just about to get within spittin' distance of that war. Those stone-faced gents look as though they're one of the factions takin' part in this dispute.'

'There you go, pard, frettin' again,' Murdoch chided. 'There's no need for us not to tell the boss man of those boys who and why we're here. Then he'll know that we ain't takin' sides in his war. Then they'll be on their way lookin' for someone else to shoot at, you'll see. That's if you don't flash that shotgun of yours about,' he warned, knowing well Skeeter's hair-triggered temper against anyone he thought was crowding him for no reason at all.

The seven riders drew up in a tight half ring around Murdoch and Skeeter. Six of them wore range clothes and were double-armed, their rifles held across their saddle horns. The seventh rider, an older man with long grey hair, favoured wearing a yellow duster and wide-brimmed straw hat. The boss man Murdoch opined. The duster-clad rider gave them a suspicious, hard-eyed look and edged his horse right close to Murdoch forcing the big regulator to step back until he could feel the heat of the camp-fire on the seat of his pants. Murdoch heard Skeeter growl and saw the skirt of his hide coat flap. He stepped quickly in front of him, smiling fit to burst at the old rider. Before he could speak, Skeeter shouldered him aside, his shotgun, both hammers at full cock pointed at the horse.

'Mister!' Skeeter grated. 'I reckon you're either Sharpe or Warren but whoever you are if you don't back that horse of yours off my pard I'll blow it into pieces of crow bait, along with your right leg. This is open range and we've every right to be here without bein' hassled by a bunch of bully boys who should be tendin' cows.'

Sharpe rocked back in his saddle with outraged amazement as though he had been struck by an invisible fist. Murdoch groaned softly as he heard the ominous clicks of shells being levered into Winchester firing chambers. Skeeter had called the tune, wrongly, he thought, but it was up to him to stand by his partner. It looked like being a short, rough shindig. The sweat trickling down Murdoch's back wasn't all caused by the nearness of the fire.

Sharpe regained his composure, and face as though hacked out of a block of timber, he leaned over in his saddle and eyeballed Skeeter. 'Mister,' he said, his voice matching the hardness of his visage, 'my boys have their long guns aimed at you, do you think you can blow them into crow bait as well?'

'Mister,' replied Skeeter, holding the rider's gaze, 'This dispute is between me and you. If it has to be settled the hard way what your boys do afterwards is their business. But by then you and me will be past carin' what the hell they do.'

Sharpe wasn't a man to allow himself to be intimidated, lose control of a situation of his own making, certainly not when the odds were stacked high in his favour. Not until now that is. The small, weasel-faced bastard was fierce-eyeing him with such intensity it was giving him the chills. And it wasn't the mad-assed glare of a gun-crazy freak but the steady, soul-seeking stare of a man who had made a decision and would carry it out come what may.

With some difficulty Sharpe swallowed his pride, though his face didn't show it. He clicked his tongue and jerked at his reins and his horse stepped back a few paces. Murdoch shifted away from the fire and began to breathe more easily then thought it was time to back up Skeeter.

He took a closer look at the boss-man's horse and saw the brand marks of the Bar Z burnt on its flank. 'Put down that gun, Skeeter,' he said. 'Mr Sharpe seems willin' to speak with us and, as you've often said, you don't want us to get involved in his trouble. Me and my pard are Cattlemen's Protective Association agents, we're carryin' papers to prove that, if you doubt my word. We're investigatin' some cattle rustling at the W Y ranch.'

Sharpe nodded. 'I know of the widow Gale,' he said. Though he still doubted that the pair were regulators. Yet the little man had shown an aggressive side to him that didn't fit in with his down-at-the-heel appearance.

'I suppose she'll vouch for who you said you were?'

'We've explained who we are!' Skeeter butted in angrily. 'We ain't used to havin' our word questioned, mister.' He had slipped the shotgun back into his pocket but he hadn't cooled down any. 'You boys oughta know what trouble you could be lettin' yourselves in for if you gun us down!' he shouted across to the ranch-hands. 'We are C P agents, regulators, and we've got the written right to apprehend, shoot, or hang any man we suspect of cattle-liftin'. We don't have to mess about with judges and juries and execution-ers!' Skeeter paused for breath, he hadn't spoken at such length before, and with so much feeling. Still angry he started his ranting again.

'Now I know your boss has got you involved in a feud where hard-workin', poorly paid ranch-hands are killin' other such-like men as though you ain't got the savvy you were born with, but killing two regulators on open range

156

will brand you as rustlers in the Association's eyes. Every agent in the north-west will be down here as fast as their horses can make it and there won't be enough trees hereabouts to hang you all. Think well on it, boys. Is a dollar a day and four squares fair recompense for all that grief?'

Skeeter thin-smiled up at the frozen-faced Sharpe. 'It ain't like shootin' down a sheriff in some backwoods town, Mr Sharpe.'

Murdoch could see that his partner's words, strung together good enough for the little fire cracker to run for congress, had caused uncertainty among the crew. Some had lowered their rifles and were muttering among themselves. Though Sharpe, he opined, would take some unsettling, the feud ran through his bloodline. Things could still turn nasty for him and Skeeter.

'And me and my pard have more than a gutfeelin',' continued Skeeter, 'that the lawman you gunned down had damn all to do with the killing of your straw boss, so in my book you're nothin' but a cowardly murderer! Ponder on that, Mr Sharpe!'

Sharpe's ramrod-back stance weakened and his face drained of blood as the invisible fist struck him another low blow. Sharpe was definitely unsettled. Confused-eyed, he could only mutter, 'How do you know . . . ?'

Skeeter pushed the knife in deeper. 'You just believe it mister. And m'be, if you've got a conscience, and the balls, you'll admit you went off at half-cock and got good men shot down like animals. You and that other crackpot Warren, could put an end to this madness.' Skeeter gave him a sneering look. 'Why, the pair of you ain't no better than Injun chiefs leadin' their tribes agin each other. But those wild, bare-assed boys ain't got the benefit of the Bible to guide them in their ways like we Christians have.'

Sharpe couldn't meet their gaze. Without saying a word, he pulled his horse's head round and dug his heels savagely in its ribs to gallop back along the trail to White Oaks. His men followed in his dust trail.

'You sure sent Sharpe off in a thinkin' mood, Skeeter,' Murdoch said. 'Though I was a mite scared that your bold-ass talkin' to him was about to send us both knockin' at the Pearly Gates.' He shot a sidelong quizzical glance at Skeeter. 'Would you have shot that fine piece of horse flesh?'

Skeeter gave him a hurt-eyed look. 'I ain't without feelin's, Murdoch. I had no intention of killin' that critter. Mr Sharpe was goin' to catch both barrels of lead shot in his hide. As you know, I believe in live and let live.' Skeeter continued. 'That don't apply to rustlers and other types of owlhoots of course, but it riles me no end to think that arrogant sonsuvbitches like Sharpe and Warren believe they have the God-given right to get men killed just to satisfy their own selfish interests.'

'Yeah, m'be so,' interrupted Murdoch, not wanting his partner to start off preaching again. 'But our business is to rope in that other arrogant sonuvabitch Mr Kingsley, and his cattle-liftin' crew. How we're goin' to do that will send us both into a deep-thinkin' mood. And we won't do it jawin' here.' He began toeing dirt on to the fire to deaden it.

14

As they rode to their hide overlooking the Circle T, Murdoch, dozing in his saddle, heard Skeeter call out, 'Rider comin' along our back trail!' He came fully alert and twisted round and saw the lone rider coming up to them fast.

'Why if it ain't the stompin' man, Mr Sharpe himself! I can't see any of his boys ass-kickin' it behind him.' He gave Skeeter a raised-eyebrow look. 'It looks like he wants to have a talk to us.'

Both of them drew their mounts round to face the incoming rancher, Skeeter pulling out his shotgun. 'It don't do to take chances, Murdoch,' he warned. 'Sharpe was mad angry enough to gun down a lawman. We made him lose face in front of his crew, killin' us could give him back his warped pride.'

Sharpe jerked up his mount in a billowing dust-raised cloud. Catching sight of Skeeter's shotgun he said, 'There isn't any need for that, none of my men is following me, I'm here to talk.'

Skeeter took in the rancher's dull-eyed, haggard-faced look and pushed the shotgun back into his pocket. 'We're listening,' he said.

'It isn't easy for me to ask for favours,' Sharpe said, his gaze looking everywhere but at the two regulators. 'I'm used to giving out orders', he continued. 'But I'd be obliged if you'd tell me who did gun down my straw boss. You did say Sheriff Price had no hand in it.'

Murdoch guessed that Skeeter's tirade against Sharpe had struck deep into his conscience. Here he was, a man, as he had just said, used to having men jump to carry out his commands, having to plead with men who had already forced him to back down in front of his crew. Sharpe was eating crow and not ashamed of showing it. Murdoch almost felt sorry for him. He gave Skeeter the nod to answer the rancher's plea. Skeeter was more skilled than he was in forked-tongued talk.

'Your foreman was killed by a gunman called Coster,' Skeeter began. 'Coster was aimin' to gun down the sheriff who was about to run him outa White Oaks, but somehow your man got in the way of the shot.' Skeeter gave the rancher an altar boy's wide-eyed innocent look as he continued his lying. 'Ill luck got your straw boss killed, Mr Sharpe.'

'This Coster,' Sharpe asked, anger hardening his face, 'is he still in White Oaks?'

Murdoch favoured him with a devil's smile. 'Sort of, but he ain't above ground.' He then began to do some untrue talking of his own. 'For no reason at all, plain cussedness I reckon, he pulled a gun on my pard here while we were visitin' the cat house and he had no choice but to put him down, for keeps.'

'So you see, Mr Sharpe,' Skeeter

said. 'There ain't no need for you to go on frettin' and worryin' about seekin' blood for the killin' of your man.' His voice iced over. 'Save your frettin' for the innocent lawman you gunned down and the men who have been killed since you started up this crazy feud again.' He gave the rancher a long, disdaining look before saying, 'Let's go, Murdoch, we've got a bunch of rustlers to track down. We've told Mr Sharpe what he wanted to know, though I reckon it didn't make pleasant listenin' for him, but you can't alter what's already happened.' He pulled his horse around and heeled it into a canter.

'My pard don't look like one of those philo-sophy fellas who write in those fancy books about what's wrong with the world, but he spouts a whole heap of good sense. Kinda makes a man think what he's doin' has been for the best. Me and Skeeter like to think that we're doin' what is right by ropin' in nogood cattle-lifters.' Murdoch's look at Sharpe as he turned his horse away from the rancher was as harsh as Skeeter's had been.

Sharpe remained stationary on the trail for several minutes. He had been doing a lot of thinking and wondering before he had caught up with the regulators. His wondering was no longer necessary now he knew who was responsible for Cullum's death but his thinking hadn't, it had only just began. What the little regulator had said about past events couldn't be changed was true, but future happenings could be stopped before they started. Enough killing had been done, Sharpe thought. And all based on his wrong assumptions. Though Warren had a big say in what could happen in the future and he might think otherwise. Somehow he had to try and have a meeting with Warren without getting himself shot, his peace of mind would not come otherwise. Sharpe, when he finally rode back along the trail to White Oaks, had a straightness in his shoulders that had not been there on the ride out.

15

Kingsley was overseeing the rebuilding of the house though his mind was elsewhere. He was still trying to figure out for sure that the hands who had torched his house were the same hands that had killed Coster. He had sent Duggan into White Oaks to probe a little deeper into the shooting of Coster. He had to find out if his wild theory was true and do something about it. Time was running out fast for him, the widow should have been long gone from her land by now.

When Duggan had reported back he told him that according to the deputy sheriff the whore who had been entertaining Coster spoke of two men whom she had never seen in White Oaks before, bursting into the room and gunning down her client. 'Though she did tell the deputy, boss,' Duggan said, 'that one of them had a knife scar down his right cheek. The deputy reckons the two men musta rode with Coster one time and had come to White Oaks to settle up an old disagreement they had with him.'

That could be true Kingsley thought. Coster was a man who would naturally collect a lot of enemies. His sixth sense, gut-feeling, whatever, wouldn't accept that reasoning. His thinking that Coster's death and the burning of his ranch house were not unrelated incidents was growing into a sure fact.

Kingsley swore out loud. Somehow the sons-of-bitches had got wind of his plans to be the big man in the territory and were trying their damnedest to scotch his grand plans. But who were they? And where were the scar-faced man and his partner now? Kingsley glanced nervously all around him. The unknown sons-of-bitches were giving him the shakes.

As Duggan had said on the night of the fire, they couldn't be any of the W Y crew. Though that didn't mean that the widow hadn't asked for help to prevent her cattle from being stolen. She hadn't the money to hire a couple of gunmen so that help could only have come from the Cattlemen's Protective Association. Kingsley now firmly believed that two of the association's agents had sneaked into the territory. And he had to admit they were good if they had discovered he was behind the cattle rustling at the WY, and that Coster had been hired by him to kill Sharpe's foreman. Kingsley smiled, not a very humorous one, but the first since the night of the fire. He had read somewhere that knowing your enemy was a battle half won. He called out for his straw boss and when Duggan came up to him he gave him his orders.

'You're going to have to make another trip into White Oaks.' he said. 'Find out all you can about the shooting of Coster. Question the whore he was with.' His face hardened. 'Real close. See if she's telling all she knows about the gunmen. I've a gut feeling, Duggan, that the men who shot Coster, and started the fire, are regulators. Asked to come here by the widow Gale.'

'Regulators!' gasped Duggan. His blood chilled. First he had thought it was vigilantes who were breathing down their necks, now it was regulators. Those bastards were as dogged and as ruthless as any vigilante in tracking down rustlers and dispensing their quick necktie justice. If they had gunned down Coster and set fire to the big house then they were the wildest regulators he had ever heard of.

He would definitely question her real closely. He would beat the hell out of her if he thought she was holding something back about the shooting of Coster.

★   ★   ★

Duggan knocked at the door of room four in the whorehouse. 'I paid for a coupla hours with you, Gloria,' he said loudly. 'Open the door; I'm kinda keen to get my money's worth.'

By casual asked questions in the bar about the shooting of Coster, still a talking topic in the town, he had got the name of the girl who had been with Coster when the gunman's luck had ran out.

Gloria unlocked her door and opened it, half-undressed for business, eyes glinting invitingly. Then her skin-deep, welcoming look turned to one of shock and fear as her client pressed a knife under her chin forcing her head back. Duggan manhandled her into the room, back-heeling the door shut behind him.

Fierce-eying her, he snarled, 'You tell me all you know about those two fellas who gunned down Coster. And I mean all! Or it'll go badly for you!' To add strength to his threat he pricked the girl with the point of his knife.

Gloria's head jerked further back as she gave a stifled scream of fear. 'I-I told the deputy all about the shooting, mister!' she managed to gasp. 'There ain't anything else to tell!'

Duggan was all set to believe her until, as frightened as the girl was, he saw a glint of defiance in her eyes. His questioning of her hadn't been close enough. He brought the knife up and laid the full length of the blade against her left cheek.

'You didn't tell the deputy rightly what happened in this room, missee,' he said. 'But you're gonna tell me, or I'll carve up that purty face of yours so badly even a drunken Injun wouldn't take you to share his blanket.'

A petrified Gloria felt the fearsome iciness of the steel on her skin, felt something warm trickling down her cheek and prayed it was sweat. Then she broke.

'The big fella said he was a lawman but he didn't wear a badge!' Her words came babbling out. 'It was his pard, a small weed of a man, who shot Coster! And that's all I know, mister, honest to God!' Gloria comforted herself with the thought that the pair must be out of Johnson County by now, maybe as far away as Montana. Well out of reach of any trouble she may have caused them by her frightened outburst.

Duggan drew his knife away from the girl's face as he chewed over what she had told him. It didn't make sense that the two were lawmen. If they had been genuine peace officers holding warrants on Coster they would have made their presence known to the sheriff and asked for his OK to arrest a man in his town. Kingsley was right, he thought, the pair could only be regulators. By making themselves out as lawmen they had panicked Coster into making a run for it so they could shoot down the poor bastard like some dog.

Then Duggan had another thought. They had been the sons-of-bitches who had fired on him and the boys, wounding Peckham, not the W Y crew. And they must be still out there someplace because they hadn't finished with the Circle T yet, not till they had seen every hand on the ranch, and the boss, strung up for cattle-lifting. That thought gave Duggan no joy at all. He bared his teeth in a wolf-like grimace. The sooner he got back to the Circle T the sooner he could set up a big hunt to track them down. The bastards had lost their edge of surprise; they could be identified. He stepped back from the girl and walked out of the room.

Gloria dropped back on to the bed, as sweat-dripping and exhausted as though she had just finished a heavy session pleasuring a whole ranch's crew. A man had been shot dead in her room, another one threatened to carve her up. Whoring, Gloria, opined, was becoming a dangerous profession.

★   ★   ★

Kingsley listened in hard-faced silence to Duggan's account of what he had learned about the killers of Coster. 'The sonsuvbitches are regulators, Duggan,' he said. 'I'm certain of it! And they're making war on us! It's time we took part in that war!'

'I intend doing just that, boss,' replied Duggan. 'I'm about to set up a hunt for the bastards. But I can't have the boys neglecting their chores too long to go ranging across the territory trying to cut their sign. The regulators musta been out there a coupla weeks and none of the line men has seen any strangers on the range.'

'We won't have to pull men off their duty, Duggan,' Kingsley said. 'I'd bet this ranch that the pair are sitting within rifle range of us, watching all that's going on here. We'll be as sneaky as them, or at least Jimmy Two Crows will.' Kingsley smiled. 'The 'breed reckons he has Sioux blood in him; now he'll get the chance to prove it.'

*　*　*

It was an hour after full dark and a stripped to the waist Jimmy Two Crows, his hatchet-carved face painted for war, was getting his final orders from his boss.

'I don't think you'll have to scout far, Jimmy,' Kingsley said. 'The pair will be holed up some spot where they can keep the ranch under observation. I'd like one of the bastards taken alive so he can tell me if he's passed on what he knows about our actions against the W Y to his superiors. But if you're forced to kill them both, do it! Understand?'

Jimmy Two Crows grunted his understanding.

'And you, Duggan,' continued Kingsley, facing his straw boss. 'Take a couple of good men as backup for Jimmy. Those two regulators are good and it's best not to underestimate their capabilities. But don't cramp Jimmy's style.' Kingsley looked at the 'breed again. 'OK, Jimmy, get hunting!'

16

'I'll have to take a stroll, Murdoch,' Skeeter said. 'Those cold beans are raisin' hell in my guts. If Kingsley don't make a move against the widow's spread soon so we can catch him breakin' the law I'll be regularly breakin' wind loud enough to be heard in the Injun lodges up there along the Bighorn.'

Murdoch and Skeeter were facing another ball-freezing night on the lookout ridge close-eying the Circle T crew.

Murdoch grinned. 'I'm missin' the widow's cookin' myself, Skeeter. But we oughta be able to catch up on our sleep when you get back. The only activity down there has been the night line riders goin' out to spell the day men at the herds.'

Jimmy Two Crows began his tracking

a quarter of a mile west of the ranch. Before he had set out on the hunt he had scanned the lie of the land and came to the opinion that the western rock and brush-covered high ground was the ideal territory where men could keep a watch on the ranch without showing themselves.

In long, loping strides he zig-zagged across the reverse slope of the nearest ridge to the ranch, making height all the time. It was too dark to pick up any tracks two riders would have made but not too dark to pick up smells. Jimmy Two Crows didn't expect to smell camp-fire smoke, the men he was hunting wouldn't be so foolish enough to light a fire, though they had horses, and horses sweat, and their droppings smell high. With the wind blowing down from the rimline Jimmy was confident that enough of his mother's Sioux blood flowed through his veins for him to pick up such-like give-away smells.

Jimmy Two Crows' perseverance paid

off. On his last cutting across the side of the ridge, just below the true crest, he caught the smell of horses and their droppings. And was close enough to them to hear their snuffling and snorting and the clink of a restless iron-shod hoof striking against a stone. Jimmy grinned, and silently thanked his long dead mother.

A cold, miserable minded Murdoch sat huddled up in a blanket, watching the lights go out in the Circle T big house, leaving only the lantern hanging above the bunkhouse door lit. He shivered as the damp night wind picked up, and he drew the blanket tighter about him. He opined he was getting too old for these cold-camp stake-outs. It could bring on an attack of the screwmatics, leaving him too stiff and painful in the joints to get up on a horse without a great deal of help. Murdoch had never heard of regulators chasing after rustlers on foot. He would need a stick to keep up with a herd of slow-moving grazing woollies.

Jimmy Two Crows bellied his way over the ridge, as silent as a shadow. Just ahead of him he saw the bulky shape of a squatting man. He took a quick glance round but couldn't locate the second regulator. Jimmy gave another Indian-like grin. His mother's spirits were sure looking kindly down on him. He drew his pistol, Mr Kingsley was about to get his regulator for questioning.

Some life-preserving instinct made Murdoch sense his imminent danger. He swung round, hand grabbing for his pistol. His attacker's pistol came down hard on his head. Murdoch saw a split-second of bright light then total darkness and without even a groan he slumped sideways to the ground.

Jimmy Two Crows cast another look around him, face all Indian, before slipping his pistol back into its holster. Moving quickly, he grabbed the ankles of the cold-cocked regulator and began dragging him down the slope. Halfway down, sweating with the exertion, he heard a low-voiced call of, 'Is that you, Jimmy?'

'I've got one of 'em, Mr Duggan,' Jimmy answered. 'he's still out for the count. The sonuvabitch is as heavy as a longhorn steer.'

'Good work,' replied Duggan. 'Me and the boys will take him off your hands. You get back up that ridge and wait for this bastard's pard.' The straw boss grinned. 'You needn't raise a sweat to haul him down, the boss only wanted one to talk to.'

Jimmy Two Crows' teeth flashed white in the dark. 'I ain't ever killed a white-eye before.'

Before Skeeter began the climb back to the lookout he walked along the foot of the ridge, stopping every few paces to listen, and peer into the deeper darkness of the valley floor. Skeeter was a born worrier. Whereas Murdoch would rely on brute force to barge his way through a hairy situation like some charging buffalo, he would, if he had time, contemplate the possible actions of an enemy and think of a counter-action. Like right now. He wasn't fully accepting Murdoch's assumption that Kingsley and his crew were all tucked up in their bunks for the night. They had given Kingsley three smacks in the eye — stopped him raiding the W Y, setting fire to his fine house, and shooting his hired gunman. Even a less proud man than Kingsley wouldn't sleep at all from thinking of what action he would take against whoever it was frustrating his grand plans.

After twenty minutes or so of prowling around in the dark and hearing or seeing nothing that caused him the slightest of uneasiness, Skeeter had to admit that Murdoch was right, even the unjust slept sometimes.

On the way up to the ridge Skeeter stopped to check on the horses, bedded down in a cave-like hollow just below the crest. To his surprise he could feel his horse, a mare, shivering, and when he reached out a comforting hand he felt the stickiness of sweat on her flank.

Skeeter cursed softly and dropped swiftly to his knees, keeping the horses between him and the rimline. His shotgun was out, hammers at full cock; he was worrying for real now. Someone had thrown a scare into his mount and that someone had to be more Indian than white man.

Two years ago while he and Murdoch were in hot pursuit of a bunch of cattle-thieves along the Montana/Canadian border a Sioux war party bushwhacked them. Only the fact that they were closing in on the rustlers and he had his shotgun resting across his saddle saved his and Murdoch's scalps. They burst through the ambush, but not before he had caught an arrow in his left shoulder, and his horse a deep, long knife slash on her right back leg.

Skeeter didn't know if horses had sixth, seventh or what senses, all he knew for certain was that from that day any Indian, old, young or male, female who came within yards of his mare, caused the horse to have the sweats and shakes. Even friendly Indians working as scouts for the cavalry. He didn't think Kingsley had a full-blood Indian on his payroll, but he could have a part Indian working for him, with enough Indian blood in him to get the jump on Murdoch. And the mixed-blood bastard would be sitting up there now, waiting, hoping to get himself another white-eye scalp.

The anger inside Skeeter was cold and controlled but every bit as revenge-seeking as a hot-blooded eye-for-an-eye get-even rage. He knew someday that either his or Murdoch's luck would turn bad. In their dangerous profession the odds couldn't always stay in their favour. That didn't mean the surviving partner had to take to his bed mourning his loss. There was the evening up of the score to be carried out. Skeeter remembered as a young boy listening to a hell and damnation backwoods preacher ranting on about the fearful plagues inflicted on the Egyptians. He cold-smiled. By thunder, he thought, Kingsley and his cattle-rustling crew were about to suffer some more up-to-date pestilences, such as house burning, stampeding cattle, hands getting bushwhacked, until the Circle T was no longer listed as a cattle ranch.

He had worried about being drawn into a feud and now by hell he was starting one of his own. Murdoch must be laughing fit to bust from the other side of his grave. First though, before he sicced the plagues on Kingsley, he had to deal with the Indian-blood man who had done for Murdoch.

Nose to the dirt Skeeter crawled his way along the top of the ridge, coming on to the lookout post from the ranch side of the high ground, the opposite way he reckoned the ambusher would be watching. Skeeter didn't want to get the same treatment as Murdoch as soon as he had cleared the crest. He also hoped that rattlers slept at night. Somewhere close by was a two-legged rattler; he didn't want the genuine article to rear up out of the grass and spit in his eye.

He had pocketed the shotgun and in his right hand he gripped a short-handled hatchet the steel head of which had been honed sharp enough to shave with. The killing had to be done quietly, allowing him time to get back down to the horses, taking Murdoch's body with him, if he could manage to lift his dead partner's great weight without the alarm being raised. The Indian would have back-up within calling distance. Skeeter stopped his crawling; it was time to show a part-Indian an Indian trick. He put a cupped hand to his mouth and gave a turkey gobbling sound then waited with the hatchet poised ready to speed it on its deadly way.

Jimmy Two Crows grinned. The big man's partner was coming in, right on to his knife. He raised himself slightly and gave an answering call back.

He didn't make an ideal target for Skeeter but the regulator knew he hadn't the time to make the man show himself more clearly or he could end up like Murdoch. He swung his arm round and the hatchet seemed to take wings. Jimmy Two Crows heard a puzzling fleeting whirring sound and, before his brain could register what it was, the steel blade sliced deep into the side of his neck. He gave a choking, gurgling sound and dropped back flat on to the ground again, as he drowned in his own blood.

Skeeter was up on his feet and ran the few yards to the man Kingsley had sent to kill him. He bent over the body and gave a satisfied grunt. He was as dead as any man could be. He grinned wolfishly. 'You weren't to know, pilgrim,' he said, 'that me and my pard don't exchange bird calls. A trick got you dead. Something to fret over down there in Hell.'

Skeeter retrieved his hatchet and after wiping it clean on the dead man's coat slipped it back into his belt. Then he began to search around for

Murdoch's body, all the while keeping an alert ear for sounds of a second ambusher. Unless Kingsley had another Indian blood man working for him Skeeter couldn't see any pigeon-toed cow-hand walk light-footed across rough ground in the dark.

When he couldn't find Murdoch's body Skeeter had to do some re-thinking. Murdoch, he thought, could only be held prisoner down there in the big house, so his one-man vendetta was no longer an option, not until he had effected a rescue of Murdoch. Or, he thought grimly, got them both killed in the attempt. Skeeter hadn't the time to come up with a grand plan on how he was going to get his partner from out of Kingsley's ranch house. Within twenty, thirty minutes, the rancher could get impatient and send men up on to the ridge to find out why there was a delay in the bushwhacking of the partner of the man he was holding in his big house. Once they came across the ambusher's body, the whole of the Circle T crew would be turned out seeking his blood. He would get his feud, but not on his terms. And, if Murdoch, as he hoped, was still alive, could get him shot out of hand as revenge for the killing of the Circle T hand.

His raid had to be carried out sneaky-like but quickly, and both of those actions depended on the situation in the big house. Though Skeeter thought there was no use worrying about that until he stepped into the house. He had to concentrate on getting close to the house fast without raising the alarm. He knew for a fact now that Murdoch had been wrong in his thinking that, apart from the night men, the rest of the ranch crew had been asleep. The son-of-a-bitch, Kingsley, had fooled them; all his men were ready to go man-hunting. Skeeter came down from the ridge on his horse, rein-leading Murdoch's mount, in a leg-breaking-risking speed. He dismounted and tethered both horses in the darkness of a barn wall then made for the fire-damaged rear of the house with his shotgun in his hands. If he hit trouble he would down as many of the Circle T crew as he could before they shot him to pieces, not fulfilling his promise feud against the ranch but at least Kingsley and his men would pay a high price in blood for their rustling activities.

★   ★   ★

Murdoch had regained consciousness with a mule kicking its way out of his head and found himself roped tight in a chair in what he took, judging by the dark wood-panelled walls and big oak desk and easy chair, to be Kingsley's den. There was no one else in the room, but he heard the sound of several voices drifting through the part open door that led into another room. In spite of the pain from his throbbing head and his hurt pride for being outfoxed, Murdoch worried about how Skeeter was making out. The man who had cold-cocked him up there on the ridge was good but Skeeter, he knew, wouldn't be so easy to jump unawares. Though he had to consider Skeeter could get careless — he had.

Murdoch began to dirty-mouth, long and loudly. The whole of the Circle T must be up and about, how wrong he had been telling Skeeter they could look forward to a good night's sleep. Then he let loose with another string of profanity that by thinking like some Eastern greenhorn he could have got his partner killed, or sitting roped up in a chair alongside him waiting for Kingsley to decide their fate. And Murdoch didn't doubt that would be a bullet in their heads.

Yet looking on the positive side, no ranch-hand had come into the room smirking, dragging in an unconscious Skeeter, or telling him he had been shot dead so the cunning little so and so must still be eluding the sons-of-bitches out there.

The first man to enter the room was Kingsley himself and he wasn't smirking. Murdoch met the rancher's hard-eyed look with a drop-dead glare of his own. 'You and that partner of yours have caused me a whole heap of unnecessary trouble,' Kingsley said. 'We haven't roped him in yet, but we will. While we're waiting you can tell me if you've passed on that I'm involved in the rustling of the widow's cattle to your superiors in Montana. I know you're both Cattlemen's Protection agents. When you were searched, papers stating who you were were found in your pocket. If you're forthcoming with this information then I'll give you a quick death, by the bullet.' Kingsley wolf-smiled. 'If the cat's got your tongue I have a tree out front that has a branch strong enough to bear your weight dangling on the end of a hanging rope. Slow choking to death isn't the choice to die I would make, Mr Murdoch.'

'Was the fella who jumped me an

Injun, Mr Kingsley?' Murdoch asked. 'While I'm dancin' on air, it'll worry me no end thinkin' that a dollar-a-day cowhand got the best of me.'

Kingsley looked at his prisoner in wide-eyed disbelief. 'What the hell does it matter who captured you?' he growled. 'And I take it you're not going to talk.'

'Oh, it means a great deal to me,' replied Murdoch angrily. 'If I'm goin' to die it kinda hurts my professional pride as a top association agent, that it's because some run-of-the-mill ranch-hand sneaked up on me.'

Murdoch knew that some day he would fall to a rustler's bullet in the heat of a shoot-out but had lost no sleep on that grim fact. It was a high-risk business he and Skeeter were engaged in. But a slow, undignified death swinging on the end of a rope was another matter, it scared him somewhat. Though not enough to let it show in front of the son-of-a-bitch standing over him.

Kingsley shook his head, lost for words. He was listening to a crazy man talk. The fat man was worrying about his hurt pride within minutes of having a hemp noose slipped around his neck. If his partner was as crazy-minded no wonder the pair of them had run rings round his crew. Before he could speak Duggan came into the room.

'We ain't heard a word from Jimmy Two Crows for over thirty minutes since he knocked out that bastard.' Duggan glared at Murdoch. 'I reckon I should take some of the boys up on to that ridge to check on him.'

Murdoch had to try hard to keep his laughter from bursting out in his face. All they would find up there would be Jimmy Two Crows' body. In that half-hour they hadn't heard from him, Skeeter had killed him. Skeeter was still running loose out there and, knowing his little partner's tetchy nature, running wild and loose. It wouldn't be as easy to drag him under the hanging tree as Kingsley thought.

Kingsley caught the glint of a look in his prisoner's eyes that disturbed him. He got the feeling the fat man was laughing at them. Although he had captured one of the agents and having the other one hunted down, he didn't seem to be in control of the situation.

'You do that, Duggan,' he said, not taking his eyes off his prisoner. 'I'll come with you. But send a hand in to stand guard here.'

Duggan couldn't understand why Kingsley needed someone to watch over a man trussed up tight who was going no place until it was time to string him up. Then he noticed the prisoner's smug-faced look. What was he so happy about when he was as good as dead? Duggan began to get the same unsettling feeling as his boss. Was the big son-of-a-bitch smirking because he had somehow figured out that his partner had done for Jimmy? Duggan tried hard not to believe that thought.

'I'll send Peckham in, boss,' he said. 'Either that fella roped up there, or his buddy, put that slug in Peckham's hide. He'll guard him real close.'

'Tell him,' Kingsley said, 'if the fat man so much as breaks wind out of turn he has to shoot him.' He brought his stone-eyed gaze back on to Murdoch. 'You may be harbouring wild hopes, mister, but that's all they'll be. I've got over twenty armed men within calling distance from my front porch, all ready to gun down your pard if he's crazy enough to come within shooting distance of this house.'

'Mister,' Murdoch said under his breath, 'you don't know just how crazy my pard can get when he gets riled. But you'll soon find out.'

After Duggan had left to get the men organized for the sweep on the ridge, Kingsley remained silent, only glaring the hate he was feeling towards Murdoch. Murdoch could see by the nervous tic pulsating in the rancher's right cheek that in spite of having a small army close by, boss man or not, he was showing fear and uncertainty.

Murdoch relaxed in the chair, stone-faced, waiting for Skeeter to make his move to rescue him, which the little hellion would try to do as sure as day followed night, not worrying too much that Skeeter's actions could get him shot by whoever was guarding him. That, thought Murdoch, with grim reality, was a cleaner way to go than having that bastard Kingsley string him up.

A ranch-hand came into the room, a thin sour-faced man who walked with a pronounced limp. He scowled at Murdoch and eased his pistol in its holster. For the second time Murdoch had a brief joyous thought. This was the fella he had wounded, badly, by the look of it, during the night raid on the W Y cattle. The straw boss had been right when he told him that Peckham would guard him good. The way the bastard was fish-eyeing him he had the urge to shoot him right now. Skeeter, as good as he was, Murdoch thought soberly, was facing long odds.

Though he reckoned his partner would already know that.

'You know what to do if he causes you any trouble!' Kingsley snapped at Peckham.

Peckham grinned. 'Yeah, boss, Duggan told me. It'll give me great pleasure to put a slug in the sonuvabitch's fat gut.'

Murdoch heard Duggan call out that the men were ready to move out. Kingsley gave him another hate-filled glare before walking out of his den. You and your crew are wasting their breath, he thought. Wherever Skeeter is he isn't up on that ridge. Murdoch then began to wonder how he could help Skeeter, like kicking the po-faced bastard guarding him in the balls. But the man who had roped him in the chair knew his knots. Keeping his gaze off Peckham so as not to further antagonize him and risk getting pistol whipped again he sat back in the chair, waiting and praying for the small miracle to occur.

Skeeter loose-tied both mounts at the rear of a barn then took stock of the situation. He had to sneak by the bunkhouse; he was close enough to hear coughing and the muttering of men ready to come rushing out if the alarm was raised.

Moving round the barn from where he had a clear view of the lamp-lit front of the ranch house, Skeeter saw the flurry of movement of several men and the faint shouting of orders carried by the night breeze. All the activity going on seemed happening there, which would favour his plan of entering the house by the fire-damaged rear. Skeeter bared his teeth in a fearsome grin. It was no going back time. With his shotgun sticking handy out of his coat pocket and the deadly hatchet held in his right hand, keeping in the shadows of the outbuildings, he made for back of the house as silently as a full-blood Sioux.

He had only taken a few paces when he heard the mournful hoot of an owl. He stopped dead in his tracks, waited a brief moment to make sure he had heard right then called out, low-voiced, 'Is that you, Mr Favour? It sure wasn't a genuine bird that just gave tongue.'

A grinning Billy Favour came round the corner of a tool shed. 'I thought you'd get my signal, Mr Skeeter,' he said. 'I didn't want to risk gettin' any closer to you in case you took me for a Circle T man, and cut loose at me.' Billy nodded towards the house. 'I take it that the big fella's in there.'

'That's right,' replied Skeeter. Then told Billy about Murdoch's capture and his killing of the ambusher. 'I don't know what state Murdoch's in, but bein' his pard it's kinda beholden on me to try and spring him.' He gave Billy a curious-eyed glance. 'How came you showed up here, Mr Favour?'

'The boss asked me to ride out to see how the pair of you were farin',' Billy said. 'She's frettin' about ever hirin' you. She'd rather have all her stock lifted than have men shot on her behalf. Now I'm here, what can I do to help?' Billy grinned again. 'I've got a hankerin' for the blood-rushin' old days.'

Skeeter smiled back. 'I don't want any fires started. I know it ain't goin' to be easy pullin' Murdoch outa there but goin' in, and out, Injun-like, is the only way I've a chance to do it. I've got one thing goin' for me: I reckon that most of the crew are at the front of the house. It's the bastards in the bunkhouse who've got me worried. If they spot me comin' out with Murdoch, we're both dead ducks. M'be you could oblige me by keepin' a gun on them till we get to the horses.'

Billy Favour remained silent and Skeeter was beginning to think it had been foolish, and wrong of him to ask an old man, a man he had only known for a short time, to risk his life on a crazy rescue bid, even though he craved for his old wild days.

Billy Favour finally spoke. 'I've got a

better idea. I'll draw the sonsuvbitches outa the bunkhouse.'

'How are you intendin' to do that, Mr Favour?' a puzzled Skeeter asked. 'I don't want you to start a small war, not when I'm hopin' to be movin' around soft-footed like.'

'Nah, I ain't goin' to fight any kinda war,' Billy replied. 'Just stir them up somewhat. I can do that by firin' down from that ridge with my Winchester on those fellas out front. I figure that will draw even the ranch cook to the front of the big house. Then all you've got to worry about are the men guardin' your pard.'

It was Skeeter's turn to remain silent for a while. 'It sounds OK to me, Mr Favour,' he said at last. 'But once you've *stirred* them up, you get to hell off that ridge fast!'

'You betcha!' grinned Billy 'How the hell did I keep a coupla jumps ahead of you blue-bellies durin' the war if I didn't know when it was time to cut and run for it?'

'No offence, reb,' Skeeter said. 'It's just that I'm a fella who frets a lot. I'll hold back until you open up, pard.'

'Let's do it then, pard.' Billy said. 'And good luck to both of us.'

'Amen to that,' replied Skeeter, but found that he was talking to himself. Billy had vanished.

Skeeter stepped gingerly over the loose planks and lengths of four by twos that lay strewn on the porch. The rear door of the house had not yet been fixed so it was no problem for him to get inside the building. In the darkness of the room, Skeeter glimpsed the dull sheen of pots and pans hanging on the walls and realized he was in the ranch's kitchen. Ahead of him at floor level he saw a bar of light. It was shining under the door that led to the main part of the house — and the room where Murdoch was being held prisoner.

Skeeter drew his Colt and thumbed back the hammer and gripped the hatchet tighter. Then waited, stone-faced, for the old bush raider to begin his *stirring up*. And then it came, a rapid fusillade of shots bringing shouts of alarm and the sounds of running and hollering men from behind the house. Skeeter managed a grin of sorts. Old Billy Favour had proved his worth again. It sounded as though every hand on the ranch bar the night riders had been drawn to the front of the house.

Kingsley, Duggan and the men with them, well up the slope, ate dirt fast when the rifle opened up. Duggan cursed. The smirking fat bastard they had tied up back there in the house knew that Jimmy Two Crows was dead, now *he* knew, or the fat man's partner wouldn't be pulling off shots at them.

When Murdoch heard the shooting, he wondered what Skeeter was up to. Had his partner gone crazy? Did he think he could wipe out the whole of the Circle T crew then come in stepping over their dead bodies and into the house and rescue him? Then he cursed himself for thinking such disparaging thoughts about Skeeter. It wasn't him who was doing the firing. Somehow Skeeter had got himself some help and Skeeter's diversionary tactics became clear to him. While the shooting held the Circle T's crew out front, the little hell-raiser would be creeping in the house from the rear. When Skeeter showed up he would have to try and distract the guard.

Skeeter opened the door slowly and quietly and stood for a moment or two at the beginning of a long, lamp-lit passage. He had to work fast. There were four doors, two on either side of the passage. At the far end was another door, leading, Skeeter opined, to the room overlooking the front porch of the house. If Murdoch was held captive in there then he would have no chance of pulling off a rescue. Highly alerted men were milling about outside only feet away. He would have to beat a hasty retreat and try and come up with another plan.

Peckham worried about the shooting and wondered if Kingsley needed him.

He stood undecided for a few minutes. Then, fish-eying Murdoch, he bent down and checked that the ropes binding him were secure before leaving the room to report to Kingsley.

Skeeter stood outside the first door, hoping that none of them was locked. They were heavy, solid wood doors and in no way could he shoulder them open. His rescue plan was becoming wilder by the minute. Letting the hatchet swing by its cord loop he reached out a hand to try the door knob.

The door ahead of it opened suddenly and a man stepped out into the passage with his back towards him, though only for a second or two. The ranch-hand must have sensed his presence and twisted round to face him. Swiftly Skeeter swung the hatchet. The blunt end of the axe smashed into the alarmed-looking face, splintering nose, cheekbones and teeth in a fiery spray of blood. He managed to catch the unconscious man as he folded at the knees before he hit the boards with an alarm-raising thump.

Skeeter anxiously eyed the far door. It still remained shut. So far so good, he thought, though his breathing was still rasping and shallow. He slowly pushed open the door and sidled into the room the ranch-hand had come out of, hatchet raised to deal out another fearsome blow but the room was empty apart from a pale, bloodied-faced Murdoch trussed up in a chair.

'There's a fella guardin' me, Skeeter,' Murdoch said. 'He's just left. I'm surprised you didn't bump into him.'

Skeeter gave his partner an all-toothed grin. He swung the hatchet. 'I bumped into him all right. He'll not do any guardin' for a long spell. Not till he gets rid of the headache I gave him.'

Murdoch grinned. 'Some assholes get nothin' but bad luck. He's the fella I put a slug into when we foiled that night raid.'

'Let's make tracks outa here,' Skeeter said. 'The sonsuvbitches will be breathin' down old Billy Favour's neck by now.'

'Is he the rifleman?' Murdoch gasped, as Skeeter sliced through his bonds with the hatchet.

'It was his suggestion to go up on the ridge,' Skeeter replied. 'His firin' has got the Circle T men runnin' about like headless chickens at the front of the house, allowin' me to walk in nice and easy as though Mr Kingsley had invited me in. The widow lady sent Billy out to see if we were OK. But that old goat has still got the killin' lust in his blood. Praise the Lord.'

Skeeter helped an unsteady-legged Murdoch on to his feet and handed him his pistol and armed himself with his shotgun. 'Can you walk OK?' he asked. 'You look as though you've been whacked real hard, and bein' tied up an' all . . . '

'I'll manage,' Murdoch said. 'But I must be gettin' old allowin' myself to be sneaked up on. Though I heard that the man who cold-cocked me was part Injun.' He shot Skeeter an enquiring glance. 'You bein' here tells me I shouldn't ask, but did you . . . ?

Skeeter gave him another one of his apologies for a smile. 'If he's part Injun then he's been in his happy huntin' grounds this past half-hour or so.'

Murdoch led the way out of the ranch house with Skeeter walking backwards covering the door with his shotgun. He was thinking that it hadn't turned out to be a bad plan after all, providing no one came through the door and raised hell with them.

'Watch out for the loose timber lyin' about outside,' he warned Murdoch. 'We ain't clear of this situation yet.'

They were well past the bunkhouse, their hopes rising every step they took from the house when a ranch-hand came out of a barn. He had been tending a mare having a difficult birth and had been unable to join the rush to the house. Now that the mare and foal were resting he had stepped out for a smoke, figuring that there were plenty of the boys at the house to deal with whatever trouble there was. He saw the two hurrying men and his makings dropped out of his mouth as he let out a yell of alarm.

His cry was drowned by the shotgun's blast. The force of its double discharge flung him back into the darkness of the barn.

'The horses are at the back of the barn on the left, Murdoch; get runnin', I'll catch up with you!' Skeeter said. Speedily he thumbed two fresh loads into the smoking maws of the gun and flicked it shut.

He fired both barrels again at the shadowy figures of men coming round both sides of the house and saw them scatter, winning him the few seconds it took to make it to his horse. Murdoch was already mounted and had loosened both tethering ropes. Behind them came wild shooting and equally wild shouting.

Murdoch grinned. 'We've sure cut it fine, pard.' And dug his heels into his horse's ribs. Skeeter did likewise, thundering away with shots flying close by them.

17

Billy Favour heard the shotgun blasts as he was climbing into his saddle. He cursed. He didn't know if Skeeter had run into trouble going in or coming out of the house; whatever it was it looked bad for the two regulators. Shouting on the ridge above him warned him of the danger he was in. He had helped all he could; it was time to take heed of what Skeeter had told him to do when things became too hot, get to hell out of it fast.

It was a pity things had gone wrong for them. For lawmen, Yankees at that, the pair were men with whom he'd willingly walk the line. Billy gave a twist of a grin. What was he yapping about, he thought, he had done that already. He promised himself that if Murdoch and Skeeter didn't show up at the W Y in the morning he would swing by this way again to try and find out what had happened to them. Billy's thin smile showed once more. Maybe later start another fire. Billy kneed his mount gently down on to the flat, face hard set, a bringer of bad news to the W Y.

The shot that brought down Skeeter's horse and tumbled him ass over head from his saddle to break his right leg as he hit the dirt, was fired by one of the three night riders guarding the herd nearest to the ranch buildings. The sound of gunfire had them leaving the longhorns to ride in to see if their guns were needed to beat off whoever it was attacking the big house. The men they heard riding in their direction were in one big hurry.

'Those riders are pushin' those horses too fast to be any of our boys,' one of the ranch-hands said. 'Could be the fellas who've been doin' the shootin' we heard.' He grinned. 'We can ask them about that after we've shot them down.'

Murdoch pulled up his horse in a

haunch dust-raising halt. Pausing only long enough to yank out his rifle from its boot he swung out of his saddle. He slapped the horse hard on its rump, sending it ahead in a skittering run hoping to draw the fire from the gun blazing away at them, giving him time to see how badly hurt Skeeter was. His ploy worked, he saw the gun flashes swing away from him. He ran back to the dark crumpled heap that was Skeeter and knelt down by his side, and breathed a silent thankful prayer when he heard his partner's cursing.

'I've busted my right leg, Murdoch,' Skeeter groaned painfully.

'That's a whole lot better than me havin' to sweat my balls off diggin' a hole to plant you in,' Murdoch growled. 'Now, let's get you up on to that high ground at the back of us before those bastards find out they're wastin' lead on an empty horse.'

It was no effort for him to pick up the lightweight Skeeter and lay him gently across one shoulder. Holding his rifle in his free hand he made with some speed for the darker shapes of the range of high ridges. He hoped he would stumble on some four-legged prairie scavenger's hole-up well hidden from the sure-as-hell pursuers, so he could set Skeeter's broken leg. That's as far as Murdoch could think ahead. If the hills were lacking such-like shelter and he had to keep moving, then as soon as it became light they would be easily picked up by men on horses and the death they had just escaped by the skin of their teeth would be tapping them on their shoulders again.

18

Billy Favour held off riding in until he saw Sam come out of the bunkhouse and walk across to the house for his morning meal before starting his chores. Phil would be with the herd. Bad news, Billy knew, went down badly in the daytime. To be shaken awake from a deep, well-earned sleep and told it, made it that much worse. And it had to be not too good news as he could see no signs of the regulators' horses.

Jessica Gale's face was as gaunt-looking as Billy's as he related to her and Sam, about to tuck into his breakfast, last night's events and what had probably happened to Skeeter and Murdoch.

'I shouldn't have asked for them to come here!' Mrs Gale sobbed. 'It's my fault that two fine men have been killed!' Her hand shook as she lowered the coffee pot back down on to the stove.

Sam, no longer feeling hungry, pushed his chair back and got to his feet. 'Mr Murdoch and Mr Skeeter wouldn't see it that way, boss,' he said, trying to comfort her. 'Every assignment they took on could have seen them killed. They knew that.'

Jessica Gale wouldn't be comforted and ran out on to the porch, still crying.

'Now we've got to ask ourselves some serious questions, Billy,' a sombre-faced Sam said. 'What will that sonuvabitch, Kingsley do next? And how can three rifles stop him from doing it? When he comes riding in again it won't be to offer the boss a fair price for the spread, it'll be to stomp us into the ground.'

'I ain't a quitter, Sam,' Billy said. 'The boss and you gave me the first regular job of work I'd had for years, saved me from turnin' into a worthless bum. I'll stay and fight the bastards, brush-boy style, if Kingsley takes over this place. I'll take my old Spencer and a coupla bandoliers of reloads and lie low in the badlands. Live off the land, eat grass if needs be. Every now and then I'll come sneakin' out and blow to hell every Circle T rider I frame in the long gun's back sights.'

Mrs Gale's frightened cry that riders were coming in, brought Sam and Billy rushing out on to the porch, Sam grabbing the single-barrelled shotgun from it's peg above the door.

'Jesus Christ!' Billy muttered. 'Kingsley hasn't wasted any time. And by the dust they're kickin' up he's brung most of his crew with him. He sure means business — get-it-done-quick kinda business.'

'You'd better step inside, boss,' a worried-looking Sam said to Jessica. 'Things could turn a mite rough out here.'

Jessica Gale gave her straw boss a fiery-eyed look. 'No one is going to drive me off my own porch, Sam! Whatever trouble is about to come to the W Y we meet it together!'

'They ain't Circle T riders!' Billy said, whose eyesight was still as keen as when he had to keep a wary eye open for patrols of Colonel Lane's free-staters' guerrillas closing in on their camp in the backwoods along the Kansas border country. That fella in the lead, sporting a yellow duster is Mr Sharpe, boss of the Bar Z!'

'Sharpe!' repeated a puzzled-eyed Sam. 'What business has he got with the W Y. He isn't thinking that we've been siding against him in his trouble with Mr Warren.' Then, thinking that for a man who had shot the town's sheriff dead out of hand it wouldn't need much to set Sharpe off to find out who was for or against him, he laid the shotgun up against the porch rail. Forcing a weak grin at Billy, he said, 'We don't want Sharpe to think that we're not friendly towards him.'

Billy Favour cast him a bleak-eyed look but followed Sam's lead, and kept his hand well clear of his holstered pistol.

The riders, eight of them, drew up their mounts several yards short of the house. Only Jeb Sharpe came right close in. He raised his hat to Mrs Gale and gave her a curt, 'Ma'am.' And an equally brief nod to Sam and Billy.

'I opine you know who I am, Mrs Gale,' Sharpe began. 'And I apologize for showing up at your front porch so early, and uninvited.' Sharpe cleared his throat. 'But circumstances forced me to travel before full light.'

And those circumstances, Sam thought, would be running the risk of riding slap bang into a Double X ambush in daylight.

'You are welcome at my house at any time, Mr Sharpe,' Jessica said, still not cowed by his presence, or the fully armed men he had brought with him. 'And you and your crew can step down. Though it will be quite sometime before I can make coffee for you all.'

'Thanks for your offer, Mrs Gale,' replied Sharpe, 'but I must turn down your hospitality. I am here on serious

219

business. I have heard from the two regulators in the territory that you are having rustler trouble so, if it is no offence to you, Mrs Gale, I've brought a bunch of my men to help your crew to clear the rustlers from your land, send them back across the Montana line — those of them we don't shoot or string up.'

Sam tried to take in what he was hearing. Help each other? From a man who started up a bloody feud by the shooting of a man who had no part in the dispute at all? Sharpe must have had powerful friends in the state capital not to have been indicted for murder. Then Sam thought that Sharpe must have got religion for he had never known a big rancher troubled by his conscience before. Yet something must have happened to him for him to bring men halfway across the county to help what to him was a two-bit cattle outfit.

Sharpe was trying to make amends. He hadn't yet got round to seeing Warren with a view to putting an end to the killing. He knew he would be shot dead before he got within three miles of the Double X ranch house. Delicate negotiations would have to be taken by a third, uncommitted party, of some standing in the territory. So far no man had come forward to willingly risk his life in such a dangerous enterprise.

The two regulators calling him a murderer and likening him to a no-good Indian, had struck hard at his pride. Sharpe didn't think that shooting Sheriff Price had been murder, the lawman had been armed, though he knew that was not the way the citizens of White Oaks saw the shooting. But if the regulators were right about a gunman shooting his straw boss then he couldn't deny the charge that he had, in a fit of temper, shot dead an innocent man.

Helping to clear the rustlers from the widow's land would, he hoped, cast him in a more favourable light to the townsfolk. And if he could prevail on Warren to end the feud it would stop the governor from sending in the army. Things would be back to normal.

Sam gave the rancher a hard-eyed look. 'There's no need for any of your boys to try and seek out the fellas who have been liftin' our cows, Mr Sharpe,' he said. 'We know who they are: Kingsley of the Circle T and his crew.'

Sharpe rocked back in his saddle, laughing. 'Why would Kingsley, a rancher who runs several thousand head of longhorns, want to steal cows from a — '

'Yeah, go ahead and say it, Mr Sharpe, a one-horse spread!' Sam interrupted angrily. 'It isn't our stock he wants, it's the W Y's grass and water he needs. Kingsley's aimin' to expand his herds and wants more land. By lifting the boss's cows, stock she can't afford to lose, he hopes she'll be forced to sell her land — to him at a giveaway price.'

Sharpe lost his humorous look as he gave Sam's statement some thought. Kingsley was only doing what he and every other big rancher had done when they were building up their spreads, forcing the smaller cattlemen to quit their land. Though he had never sunk so low to steal a widow's cattle.

'What my foreman said is true, Mr Sharpe,' Jessica said, her face as unyielding as Sam's. 'And much worse. Kingsley's hired gunman shot my boy, badly wounding him.'

'I'm sorry to hear that, Mrs Gale,' Sharpe said, thinking that another range war had broken out in the county, albeit a small one. But not, he guessed, to the widow and her small crew. 'He could be the same hired gun who shot my straw boss. According to the regulators his target had been Sheriff Price but shot my man by mistake.'

Sam didn't know what Murdoch and Skeeter had told Sharpe about how his straw boss had got killed, or why, other than keeping Sharpe out of their business.

'They also told me that to defend themselves while they were in White

Oaks,' Sharpe continued, 'they were forced to shoot the gunman, killed him dead.'

Sam and Billy grinned at each other. 'The pair ain't got much shine about them, Sam,' Billy said. 'But when they mention a thing they sure as hell do it.'

Sam saw the puzzled, doubting emotions sweeping across Sharpe's face. 'You haven't worked it out yet, have you, Mr Sharpe?' he mocked.

'Worked out what?' Sharpe asked irritably. 'All I know is what the two regulators told me. That Sheriff Price had no hand in the killing of my foreman. He was the gunman's target. Cullum got shot by mistake.'

Sam grinned. 'Those two characters only told you what they wanted you to know, Mr Sharpe. Ask yourself this: if Kingsley will resort to rustling and the shooting of a boy to get hold of the grass you and your boys have ridden over, what other low, dirty tricks would he be capable of to get more land and water? And do you think that a man who hires out his gun to earn his wherewithal could miss a target he's drawn a bead on? Think hard on it, Mr Sharp.'

Sharpe didn't have to ponder too long before he accepted the stomach-turning fact that Kingsley had gone to a lot of trouble just to get his hands on the widow's small stretch, but he also had his and Warren's holdings in his sights. More gut-chewing was that the son-of-a-bitch had used him to get what he wanted. He had personally killed a man and was responsible for the deaths of several other men. Sharpe shivered. Their ghosts would haunt him forever. He would never be able to ride tall in the saddle again.

Only his burning eyes set deep in a hard expressionless face showed his raging anger towards Kingsley as he swung round on his horse and faced his crew. 'Boys!' he snapped. 'See to your guns! We've got some stinking polecats to smoke out!' He turned back and looked down at Sam and Billy. 'I figure that you'll want a hand in the smoking out.'

'Our beef with Kingsley is just as personal,' Sam said. 'We'll ride with you.'

19

Murdoch winced and swore as a Winchester shell chipped splinters off one of the boulders he and Skeeter were forted-up behind. It felt as though his cheeks had been slashed with an open razor. By the angle of the shot one of the bastards must have worked his way behind them. It could only be a matter of time before he could be firing directly into the dip in the rocky outcrop. Kingsley had them well and truly by the balls. Murdoch thin-smiled. His and Skeeter's dreams of herding sheep in their old age were just what they had been — fanciful dreams. Kingsley's ring of riflemen on the hillside would see to that.

Murdoch had been lucky to spot the blackness of a fissure in a rock face part way up the hill. He had laid the unconscious Skeeter down outside it then, managing to squeeze his great bulk through the crack, found that it ran several feet into the cliff face before slanting to the left and petering out. It would have to do for the present. He walked back to the opening for Skeeter.

It was not long before Murdoch heard the voices of their hunters passing within feet of the opening, not one of the Circle T men bothering to check out the crack in the cliff face.

Its disadvantage was that it was too narrow for him to bend down and try and set Skeeter's broken leg, and it contained no water source, either by seepage from an underground spring or trickling down its walls.

When it came light and if the Circle T men had moved on, he would have to take the chance to try and find another hideout with water at hand. Right now Murdoch felt he could drink a fair-sized creek dry. He knew that when Skeeter came to he would need water urgently or he could die. He also knew that if it was Skeeter's day to die he would want it to be in the open, not like some coyote trapped in its hole.

Murdoch listened at the cave opening for several minutes. On hearing no sounds of men talking or moving around, he stepped out of the cave. He could see no signs of any of Kingsley's men either close by or down on the plain. In the daylight he could see that the hillside was broken up into several rocky features and shale slides. If there was any water on this ridge, he thought it would be among the higher rocks or maybe in pools along the ridge itself. He gave the scene another sweeping-eyed scrutiny and still spotted no movement. It was take-a-chance time. He squeezed himself back into the cave for Skeeter.

With Skeeter held firm on his shoulder with his hand that held the rifle, he had his pistol gripped in his left hand. There were fair chances and outright foolish risks to take, both of which could get them killed. But at least he was ready to bring down some of Kingsley's men with him. With a final look behind him he set off.

Several hundred feet higher, weaving his way through dangerous rock slides and round great boulders, Murdoch began to think that his and Skeeter's regular good luck was back with them. The crest of the hill was not too far ahead and once they had breasted it they would be out of sight of any Circle T riders scouring the flat.

A stretch of shale moved under Murdoch's feet causing him to slip downhill for a few feet and the shot that had been aimed to blow his head away only whizzed harmlessly in front of him. He whirled round firing as he turned at the rifleman standing between two rocks all in a brief flash of time. The rifle cracked again, firing skywards as its owner, arms outflung, staggered backwards out of Murdoch's view. Heedless of the shifting ground beneath his feet, Murdoch, in a series of wild leaps made for the shelter of a clutch of man-height boulders, his face set in a fierce grimace anticipating the painful smashing impact of a Winchester shell in his back.

He laid Skeeter down in the shallow basin formed by the rock formation then peered over the top of one of the boulders with his rifle, ready to make a fight of it. No more shots came his way so he reckoned that Kingsley had only left one of his men on the hill. That didn't alter the grim reality that the shooting would draw Circle T men from all over the range. In a few minutes' time he was proved right; he could see arrow heads of riders' dust cutting across the flat towards the high ground.

$\star \quad \star \quad \star$

The first of the Circle T men to feel the wrath of Jeb Sharpe was one of the three ranch-hands branding calves. He was first of the three to see the line of horsemen haring in on them. He grabbed for his rifle lying at his feet.

The hail of pistol shots from Sharpe's men flung him yards away from the branding fire, killing him several times over. The other two men grabbed at air.

Sharpe glared down at them. 'Take their pants, boots and guns!' he barked. 'We'll pick them up on the way back. They'll not wander far!'

In no time at all four of the Bar Z men had carried out his orders and were back on their horses. Sharpe gave them the signal to move on out then suddenly called on his men to hold it. 'Do you hear that?' he said.

'Yeah, I do,' said Sam. 'That's gunfire!' He grinned at Billy. 'That means at least one of the wild boys is still alive!'

'They sound as though they are being hard pressed,' Sharpe said. 'Ride hard, men, before it is too late to help them,' He punched at the air with his fist, the signal for a mad-ass gallop.

It was Billy Favour this time who called for them to hold it.

'It would be foolish for us to go

chargin' in, Mr Sharpe,' he said. 'Kingsley's men might outnumber your boys and his men are on high ground. We'll be sittin' ducks for them when we ride in. We're here to do the killin', Mr Sharpe, not the other way around.'

Sharpe glared at Billy, an unshaven, over-the-hill cow-hand daring to question his authority. But the hard glint in the old man's eyes and the W Y's foreman saying, 'I'd listen to him, Mr Sharpe. Billy was an expert in this kind of killing work before you and me branded our first calves,' stopped him from expressing his anger in words.

'What plan of action do you suggest then?' he said, the words coming out grudgingly. 'Time is not on the regulators' side.'

Billy grinned. 'We get ourselves some help, Mr Sharpe. And there's a whole heap of help on hand.' He swung down off his horse and picked up a lighted brand from the branding fire then ran over to the sizeable herd grazing only a few yards away. Not pausing in his stride he ran the torch through the grass behind the cattle. The nearest cows smelt the smoke and began to shuffle their feet and snort nervously. Then the smoke burst into a line of wind-driven flames and the cattle, in one bellowing roar, took off in a hoof-kicking-dirt run. Billy came hurrying back and remounted. 'Now we can go, Mr Sharpe, but keep well to the right on that hard ground. What with the smoke and the dust the longhorns are kickin' up, those sons-of-bitches won't know we're on them till they're eye-ballin' our gun barrels.'

Sam grinned. Billy was reliving his brush-boy days. He had never seen him look so cheerful.

★   ★   ★

Murdoch estimated that there were at least nine, ten rifles opposing them. He risked being killed outright or blinded by rock splinters every time he poked his rifle over the lip of the rock to fire back. He stood well clear of the boulder to concentrate on his greatest danger, the rifleman working his way across the cliff face above him. He gave a cynical grunt. What the hell did it matter who fired his and Skeeter's killing shots? In a few minutes' time Kingsley's men would come boiling over the rocks with guns blazing. Though he thought his pard could cheat the bastards yet; he could die for lack of drinking water.

He suddenly heard a rattle of loose shale and caught a brief glimpse of a leg sticking out from an overhanging rock thirty feet or so directly above him. His rifle swept up to his shoulder and he snapped off two shells. Next he saw a man's head and shoulders rear in full sight and two more shots winged on their way. Murdoch heard a high-pitched scream and a body came hurtling through the air to land with a sickening thud just outside his hole-up then tumble down the rest of the way to the flat in a disjointed arms and legs bundle, bringing down a small avalanche in its wake.

Murdoch felt like doing a small jig. Between them, counting Coster, they had finished off four of Kingsley's men. If he did not increase that tally it would still be a long time before the rancher stopped having bad dreams and cursing the day he took on the Cattlemen's Association regulators.

The Circle T gunfire increased in its intensity and Murdoch guessed that seeing their bunkhouse pal's body rolling down the hillside had goaded them into making an all-out attack. Laying down his rifle, he took the still unconscious Skeeter's pistol from him and, holding pistols in both hands, lips drawn back in a fierce, defiant snarl he waited for the overwhelming rush of killing men.

To Murdoch's surprise the firing suddenly ceased, then he heard confused shouting. Puzzled, he risked a look over the boulder, Circle T men were slipping and sliding their way down the slope. Further down, on the flat, he saw a long drifting dust haze, mixed with the black smoke of a rapidly dying grass fire and, further away, the distant thunder of a stampeding herd of longhorns. What set off Murdoch's beaming grin was the line of riflemen at the foot of the hill picking off the wildly scattering Circle T men.

He looked down at Skeeter. 'I don't know if you can hear me, pard, but, as the Good Book puts it, we've been snatched from the jaws of death by a whole bunch of men. I ain't got any idea who they are, but I don't care if they're riders from Hell and led by old Nick himself, I'll shake hands with every mother's son of 'em.'

Murdoch's joyous smile froze as the hairs on the nape of his neck bristled, a warning that came too late. He whirled round and found himself facing the muzzle of a crazy-eyed Kingsley's rifle.

'I had a grand plan!' Kingsley almost sobbed. 'And you two sonsuvbitches ruined it for me! I'm finished, but by hell, I'm taking you down with me!'

The shotgun blast deafened Murdoch and tore Kingsley's chest and face into bloody shreds, wiping out his maniacal look of hate forever as he fell to the ground.

Murdoch found himself trembling. He was getting too old for these wild back-to-the-wall situations. He gazed down at the blood-drained face of Skeeter.

'I was wondering when you were goin' to take part in this shindig,' he said po-faced. 'We're supposed to be a two-man team.'

Skeeter's face twisted in a painful shadow of a grin. 'You seemed to be doin' OK on your own, pard,' he croaked weakly. 'But when I saw that Kingsley had sneaked up on you, like that fella who laid you out did up on our lookout ridge, I thought I'd better help you out. I figure your old age is makin' your reactions slow down somewhat.'

'My thoughts exactly, Skeeter,' replied Murdoch, then found that his partner had passed out again. He bent down and picked him up. 'It's time I got you some drinkin' water and have a doc look at that leg, not forgettin' to thank the boys who got us out of this helluva tight spot.' He grinned. 'You've got careless again, that scattergun has burnt another hole in that fine coat of yours.'

Murdoch met up with Sam and Billy Favour before he reached the flat. And after telling the two anxious-faced W Y men that Skeeter was OK, apart from a busted leg and the need for a drink of water, he asked who he and Skeeter were obliged to for saving their lives.

'You'll have to thank old man Sharpe and his boys,' replied Sam. 'He brought some of his crew over to the W Y to help us to clear the rustlers off our range. Telling him how Kingsley had used him to start up the feud again really got his dander up. Him and his boys are out roping in every Circle T man they can flush out. He intends hanging 'em all. Personally put the noose around Kingsley's neck.'

'He's due for a disappointment,' Murdoch said. 'Skeeter blew Kingsley to hell just before the sonuvabitch did likewise to yours truly,' he added, soberly. 'Now I'm goin' to get Skeeter to some water before he dries out then haul him to White Oaks and get the doc to fix up his leg.'

'There's a spare bunk in the crew's quarters at the WY,' Sam said. 'And it's nearer than White Oaks, save Skeeter a lot of pain travelling.' He grinned. 'The boss's chow is a damn sight more palatable than what's served up in the eating-places in White Oaks.'

Murdoch matched Sam's grin. 'I'm partial to good chow myself. You've got youself a coupla payin' guests.'

⋆   ⋆   ⋆

It had been over two weeks since the small battle, and Skeeter, his leg on the mend, was sitting, resting on Mrs Gale's front porch, and thinking of how things had turned out. A man he had called a murderer to his face had saved his and Murdoch's lives. You couldn't have much stranger happenings than that, he thought. It made an old sinner like himself believe in religion.

He saw the bulky shape of Murdoch riding in, returning from his trip to White Oaks to wire head office that they should be able to make it to Montana in five or six days' time. Skeeter grinned. Not to quit the association and become sheepmen. As Murdoch had said, tending woollies would soon have them drawing pistols on each other just to liven things up. Cursed, or blest, they would always be hunters of cattle and horse-lifters until some bad-asses' lead put a permanent end to their calling.

A wide-grinning Murdoch dismounted, and stepped on to the porch. 'For a fella who wanted to stay well clear of the Warren and Sharpe dispute you sure did all right. You've put an end to the feud!'

Skeeter gave him a blank-faced look. 'I did? How for Chris' sake?'

'Sharpe died of a heart attack three days ago,' Murdoch began. 'The doc reckons that all the excitement of shootin' and hangin' the Circle T rustlers must have brought it on. The closest kin to Sharpe entitled to take over the Bar Z lives back East. With their boss bein' dead, the ranch crew ain't keen to carry on with the feud. And the men who went to parley with Warren told him that none of them were kin to Sharpe and that all they wanted to do was what they drew their pay for, nursin' Bar Z cows. Warren told them that as long as they did just that he wouldn't hassle them.

'If you hadn't upset Sharpe that day he came up to us on the trail by likin' him to a no-good Injun and a murderer, he wouldn't have felt obliged to ride over here and offer his help to hunt down the widow's rustlers and been on hand to save our necks. Then he gets himself dead and the feud's over. I reckon that wipes out all the hard things you said about him, Skeeter.'

Murdoch sighed. 'The Good Lord sure does move in mysterious ways, pard. And choses some unlikely fellas to do the shiftin'.'

And Skeeter, who thought that he would never see stranger things happen, opined that what Murdoch had just said was the daddy of them all. He would be glad when they were back on the hunt for rustlers again. All this ruminating was making his head spin.

Murdoch sniffed at the air. 'It smells like that chow is about ready. We'd better make the most of it, Skeeter. In a coupla weeks' time we could be back swallowin' cold beans in some godforsaken hole up along the Canadian border. I hope all this fine grub the widow's been favourin' us with ain't made us soft or we could be takin' up sheep herdin' yet.'

He followed the stick-assisted Skeeter into the house.

We do hope that you have enjoyed reading this large print book.

Did you know that all of our titles are available for purchase?

We publish a wide range of high quality large print books including:
Romances, Mysteries, Classics
General Fiction
Non Fiction and Westerns

Special interest titles available in large print are:
The Little Oxford Dictionary
Music Book, Song Book
Hymn Book, Service Book

Also available from us courtesy of Oxford University Press:
Young Readers' Dictionary
(large print edition)
Young Readers' Thesaurus
(large print edition)

For further information or a free brochure, please contact us at:
Ulverscroft Large Print Books Ltd.,
The Green, Bradgate Road, Anstey,
Leicester, LE7 7FU, England.
Tel: (00 44) **0116 236 4325**
Fax: (00 44) **0116 234 0205**

HELL TRAIL

Rio Blane

Riding in the desert, bounty hunter Frank Clooney's horse goes lame and he hitches a ride with the Carver family, using the alias Sam Rafter. But the Carver family only brings trouble: Ned Carver is a tyrant, and his wife sees Clooney as a way to gain freedom for herself and her daughter. Then outlaw Spitter Larch joins them, and if Larch remembers who Sam Rafter really is, Clooney's life won't be worth a plugged nickel!

FACES IN THE DUST

Corba Sunman

Pinkerton detective Ward Loman rode into Coldwater, Texas, hunting down the killer Leo Slattery. But there was trouble on the local range involving Leo's family, headed by Hub Slattery, owner of the HS ranch. In the worsening situation Loman rescues Kate Hesp, and is plunged into a deadly sequence of events with its origins in the war between North and South, involving the disappearance of a gold shipment. As Loman expected, gunsmoke and death would be the outcome.

CLEARWATER JUSTICE

Scott Connor

For five years Deputy Jim Lawson had wanted to find his brother Benny's murderer. So when suspect Tyler Coleman rides into Clearwater, Jim slaps him in jail. But the outlaw Luther Wade arrives, threatening to break Tyler out of jail. Then Jim's investigation unexpectedly links Benny's murder to the disappearance of Zelma Hayden, the woman he had once hoped to marry. Can Jim uncover the truth before the many guns lining up against him deliver their own justice?

BLOOD KIN

Ben Nicholas

Cole Vallantry, outnumbered and cornered, desperately swinging punches, is about ready to concede defeat — and not only regarding the brawl in the Buscadero saloon. His mission, the manhunt which had dragged him across Arizona in the blazing midsummer, is at a standstill, the trail having finally petered out. Then a tall stranger wades into the fracas, unbelievably taking Vallantry's side — but what is *his* agenda?